Jimmy and Mr. Nicholson walked back to the house. As they started up the back stairs, an all too familiar voice called Jimmy's name.

Reluctantly he turned. Mr. Krebs was glowering at the Harmons' back gate as if he were already thinking about something else.

Jimmy started to say, "The dogs were just here for the night because of the snow," when he realized Mr. Krebs was saying something about Megan. About Megan being gone.

"Gone?" Jimmy repeated. "I saw her in the window this morning."

"She's gone now," said Mr. Krebs. "Her grandmother put her down for a nap about one-thirty and when she went to wake her up, Megan was gone."

A chill clutched Jimmy. How could she be gone?

Lassie™

TO THE
RESCUE

These heartwarming stories of a boy and his beloved dog Lassie have demonstrated the values of faithfulness, loyalty, and love to boys and girls for nearly five decades. As Jimmy and Lassie face different situations through the Lassie stories from Chariot Family Publishing, these same principles will come alive for children of the '90s in a way that they can understand and apply to their lives.

Look for these Lassie books from Chariot at your local Christian bookstore.

Under the Big Top
Treasure at Eagle Mountain
To the Rescue

TO THE
RESCUE

Adapted by
Marian Bray

Chariot Books™
*A Division of Cook
Communications Ministries*

Chariot Books™ is an imprint of Chariot Family Publishing
Cook Communications Ministries, Elgin, Illinois 60120
Cook Communications Ministries, Paris, Ontario
Kingsway Communications, Eastbourne, England

Cover illustration by Ron Mazellan
Cover design by Joe Ragont Studios

First Printing, 1995
Printed in United States of America
99 98 97 96 95   5 4 3 2 1

Table of Contents

Stuck in the Snow

The last day of school before Christmas break, twelve-year-old Jimmy Harmon thought as he waited for Blake Smith to show up at the corner where they met to walk to school. He and Blake were both in seventh grade at Farley Middle School, and this past year they had become good friends.

Jimmy kicked the newly shoveled snowbank sending a flurry of snow into the air. A wisp of his ginger brown hair fell loose from his under his ski cap. *Better yet, it is only six days until I'm thirteen.* A big grin slowly crossed his face. *Thirteen*, that word had a good sound to it. Now he would finally be considered a teenager, not just a kid. He would officially be a member of the teen group at church, and just maybe he would get a little more respect.

"What are you going to do for your birthday?" Blake interrupted Jimmy's daydreaming.

Jimmy noticed that it had started to snow again. Falling snowflakes came to rest in Blake's curly black hair. Jimmy shrugged. "It's always weird because it's so close to

Christmas, you know?" Last year he'd had a cross-country skiing party with a bunch of kids from school and his youth group. It was fun.

This year was different somehow. Mom and Dad were really busy and had never even asked what he wanted to do. He didn't want to be a complaining brat, so he didn't say anything. But he wished they would mention it, so he could at least invite some kids over. It didn't matter if they didn't do much. He and his friends could just hang out. Then he thought, *I hope they remember my birthday!*

Blake, a serious looking black kid with horn-rim glasses, nodded. "That's rotten, huh? I bet a lot of people just give you one present, birthday and Christmas together."

"You know it," he said. "But Mom and Dad don't do that. They're cool about it."

"Do you know what you're gonna get?"

"I think new running shoes. I mean the cool, expensive type," said Jimmy. But as he thought about it, he wasn't even sure he'd get the shoes. That had been a conversation back in October when he had started running cross-country. Nothing had been said about it since.

Sunlight filtered through trees coated with ice. A few brave crows hung out in an elm tree, cawing so loudly that Jimmy figured if they lived in a mountainous place, instead of the flat town of Farley, Iowa, the noise would bring down an avalanche.

"What are they making such a fuss about?" asked Blake. His father was a veterinarian, so Blake noticed birds and animals more than most people. Jimmy liked that about his friend.

"Us, I guess," said Jimmy.

They walked under the tree. The three crows hollered their lungs out. Across the street was a small park. The summer picnic tables and benches were packed away and the park was a flat, square rock, like a white dinner napkin, spiked down around the edges with trees.

The park was an old friend. Jimmy often ran laps in the park with Lassie, his tricolored, rough-coat collie. Sometimes they played catch with a frisbee on the grass.

A movement caught Jimmy's attention. Today on the snowy square a horse was playfully avoiding the old man who was chasing him. It looked as if the horse was playing. Jimmy knew if he'd been trying to catch the horse he wouldn't consider it playing; he'd be mad.

The horse, the color of copper, stood so still that snow collected on her arched neck until the man was inches from her. Then she whirled in a spray of snow, and trotted away, tossing her head, as if laughing.

"Look at that," said Jimmy.

"I am looking, bro," said Blake.

"We're pretty good animal catchers, aren't we?" Jimmy asked.

"The best," Blake said.

"Let's go."

Jimmy could see the scenario unreel in his thoughts. *Man lets horse out to stretch legs. Horse gets away and won't let man catch it.* It happened all the time when his little sister had owned a pony. The pony's name was Wink, but Jimmy always called it Stink.

They ran across the street, past a deep blue Ford full-sized pickup truck with a cream-colored topper, and an open horse trailer. Briefly, Jimmy glanced at the red stenciled words "Toymaker" and a picture of a horse-drawn wagon on the side of the truck topper.

A lean, wiry old man was calling, "Now, Bess, enough is enough."

The mare coyly pawed with one front foot, tossing her snowy mane, her upper lip stuck in the air. Jimmy knew she was saying, like a little kid, "Nah, nah, you'll never catch me."

"We can help," called Jimmy as he and Blake ran up.

The old man turned gentle brown eyes on them. Jimmy could see obvious relief on the man's face as if sunlight had burst onto it.

"My name is Jimmy Harmon," said Jimmy. "And this is my friend Blake Smith. We can help catch your horse if you'd like."

The old man swept off his stained fedora hat.

14

"I would be much obliged. I'm Gabriel Nicholson, at your service, or at least I will be once I capture my errant horse. This is Bess, my Morgan mare. Bess, I must say, is in a foul temper. She hates being in the trailer more than one day in a row, so she's staging her protest."

Jimmy tried not to laugh. What a strange old guy. Kooky, but he seemed harmless enough.

"I'll go this way; you go that way," said Blake. Jimmy nodded and set down his backpack. Slowly he walked around the front of the mare rolling her eyes still, twitching her tail like a prim schoolmarm. Blake strolled around her backside.

Jimmy reached a casual hand out, not touching her. The mare backed up. Blake rocked light-footedly behind her, blocking her path. True to horse form, she shifted forward. Jimmy edged closer.

They played nontouch tag for another minute. Bess stepping one way, Jimmy or Blake blocking until they had her between them, still not touching, but very much holding her.

"Game's over, girl," said Jimmy. Bess shook her head and gave a sign as if to say, "Oh, okay, you win."

She lowered her head in resignation. Jimmy took her halter as the chilling buzz of the school warning bell jolted him.

"We're gonna be late. Gotta go," gasped Jimmy and swiftly led the mare to Mr. Nicholson. When the old man took the reigns, Jimmy sprang for his pack and he and Blake waved and bolted out of the park. Mr. Nicholson's thank yous, followed by a long whinny, trailed after them like their panting breaths.

Jimmy ran hard. Late, that's all he needed. He'd definitely get detention this time. He'd already been late twice in the last marking period. He'd thought the tardys had been for good reasons, but try and tell that to the vice principal. Who wanted detention on the last day of school? Not him. He knew that no explaining to the boys' vice principal would make any difference.

Jimmy poured on the speed, knowing that he'd never make it in time, even if he was the fastest sprinter in the school, which he wasn't. Blake flew at his heels.

Detention, here I come, Jimmy thought miserably.

2

Farley Animal Hospital and Shelter

Lassie pricked her ears after the tardy bell pierced through the cold air. In the still of the morning, the sound of the bell could be heard for several blocks.

The big collie was alone in the house. Jimmy and Sarah were in school, Mr. Harmon was at church, and Mrs. Harmon was at the discount toy store helping to sort damaged toys to be donated to the church's toy and food drive.

Lassie stood on her hind legs and carefully lifted the back door latch. She nosed the door open and slipped into the five-acre backyard, complete with an old pipe corral and a shed big enough for a horse or steer. When Sarah had a pony, the Harmons jokingly called the shed, "the barn."

At the back gate, Lassie reared up on her hind legs. Smoothly she pulled on the wire attached to the latch and opened it. Nudging the wooden gate open, she trotted down the driveway, heading into the wind where a series of interesting scents and sounds came to her on the chilled air.

Ten minutes later Lassie trotted into the park and barked softly. Mr. Nicholson turned. "Who do we have here?" he asked. He was holding a large square handkerchief against the mare's hip. It was stained with drying blood. Bess swung her head toward the collie.

Lassie sat before Mr. Nicholson, her soft brown gaze first fixed on his equally soft brown gaze, then her eyes shifted to the injured mare.

In the past Lassie had had a few of her injuries doctored in the animal hospital. She knew from the smells at the hospital that horses were also treated.

Lassie barked sharply and got up. She paced a few feet away from Mr. Nicholson. He watched the glossy collie. She barked again.

He seemed to understand. "You want me to follow you?" he asked.

She barked eagerly and pranced a little farther down the street.

"Let me get situated, girl, and we'll follow where you want us to go," said Mr. Nicholson. He taped his handkerchief to Bess's wound with broad strips of paper tape. He carefully led the mare into the horse trailer and tied the lead line securely.

Lassie stood on the sidewalk, supervising, her tail gently wagging. Mr. Nicholson opened the truck door and motioned for her to jump in. "Which will it be: You want

18

to walk or ride with me in the truck?"

Lassie barked and began running down the street.

"Have it your way. I'll follow you," Mr. Nicholson called as he climbed into the truck cab.

❦

Finally, school was over. The last bell clamored and Jimmy was out of his seat and hit the hall before the bell finished ringing. He met Blake at their locker. He hadn't seen him all day because their schedules were totally opposite.

When Blake showed up, Jimmy asked, "Were you late this morning?"

Blake shoved his books into the locker. "No. Were you?"

"Just as I sat down in my seat the tardy bell rang. I couldn't believe it. We had to have been ten blocks from school."

Blake said, "Don't knock it, bro."

"I'm not. I just can't believe we weren't late." Jimmy paused, thinking. Because his dad was a pastor, he learned early that God answered prayers, but not usually stuff like this, stuff like bailing you out of trouble that you made for yourself. If Jimmy didn't study for a test, he knew it was kind of useless to pray to get an A. Prayer just didn't work like that. Unfortunately.

"Maybe time stood still for us," joked Blake. "You know, because we were doing a good deed and all."

"I was doing a good deed both times I was late last month," said Jimmy. "But the tardy bell still caught me." They walked book free down the rapidly emptying hall.

Blake snorted. "Get real, Jim. Talking with Katie Madison was a good deed?"

"Yeah, it was. She was upset. Her Gran was on her case for no reason. She needed someone to talk to."

"Oh, and then talking to Lindsey Conner about Katie Madison was also a good deed?"

"It was! Lindsey was afraid Katie was mad at her, so she was asking me about it."

Blake gave an exaggerated sigh. "I'm in awe. You are such a dedicated friend."

Jimmy gave up explaining. Blake didn't understand about Katie anyway. Jimmy and Katie had been friends for a long time, and well, they understood each other. He had to help her out.

This morning was still kind of weird. How often do you meet a complete stranger in the city park in Farley? Especially an old man with "Toymaker" written on his truck? Oh well, he'd figured out a long time ago that life was weird, usually very weird.

At the corner of Main and Bigelow, Blake said, "Dad wanted me to stop by." He made a face. "The shelter section is full." He rolled his eyes. "Guess what that means?"

Jimmy knew. That meant all the dog runs and cat cages

20

were filled with homeless animals. "Need help?" he asked.

"Are you kidding? Do flies fly? Do ducks duck? Does Spock beam up?"

"I-I-I think I've got urgent business at home," Jimmy said hesitatingly.

Blake grabbed his arm. "Too late, you committed yourself. I appoint you my assistant." Jimmy laughed and followed Blake.

They hurried down the street, past various shops and homes decorated with Christmas boughs, bells, ornaments, angels, nativity scenes, cheery Santas and elves. Jimmy had done most of his Christmas shopping already. He was debating if he should get Katie a really cool sweater, one with a wolf howling on it; or if that was too personal, maybe he should get her . . . that was the problem. Nothing else seemed right. Mom had suggested a fruitcake! You know, a fruitcake from a fruit cake! No way!

The Farley Animal Hospital took up a whole block. Blake's Dad, Dr. Smith, was one of several vets working at the hospital. Dr. Smith drove a clean, white truck, the back compartmentalized to hold his equipment and refrigerator with medicines. He had to drive out to see most of his patients, who were pigs, sheep, cattle, horses, and other large animals. Sometimes he had surgical patients at the hospital.

Extra kennel runs were used for an informal shelter

when the county animal shelter filled up. Like now. Unlike the county shelter, the vets never put animals to sleep. Jimmy hated that term, "to sleep." The animal hospital waited patiently until the animals were adopted out to new homes.

Jimmy didn't mind helping to clean kennels. He liked seeing the different dogs, even the cats, though he wasn't a cat person. Katie had gotten her dog, Rags, at the hospital shelter and Rags was one of Lassie's best friends.

The boys went in through the back staff door. "Dad's truck wasn't in the parking lot," said Blake as they barged into the staff lounge area. "But he told me if he wasn't here to go ahead and start hosing down the cages." They dumped their jackets and gloves. Jimmy pulled off his heavy sweater. Cleaning kennels worked up a good sweat, even when it was cold outside.

The animal hospital was nearly as large as a people hospital. They walked down the covered passage from the small animal hospital to the hospital barn and the shelter. Inside the barn were two operating rooms closed off by spotless, silver double doors. Ten stalls were available. Today, one held a prize-winning Hampshire boar.

Blake pointed at the hog. "He cut a tendon in his leg trying to climb out of his pen," he said.

"Hogwash," said Jimmy, snickering at the pun. The hog just glared.

A holstein cow blinked blearily from a stall across the way. "She had this viral infection," said Blake. "It took Dad a few days to figure it out."

"Cowabunga," said Jimmy.

"Easy for you to say."

Last December Jimmy remembered that Dr. Smith had treated a camel from a traveling live nativity show. Now that had been something!

In the last stall, head hanging over the bottom of the stall door, was a copper-colored mare. She put her upper lip in the air.

"That's Bess!" exclaimed Jimmy.

A familiar, wizened face appeared from around the mare's head. Mr. Nicholson!

"Hello Master Jimmy and Master Blake. So we meet again. A small world. I trust you weren't late to school?"

Mr. Nicholson

Jimmy's face burst into a huge smile. "We weren't, thanks."

"I'm glad," said the old man.

"Is Bess hurt?" asked Jimmy.

Blake already was running his hands down the strong bones of the mare's front legs, looking like a slightly smaller version of Dr. Smith. "No swelling," he murmured. Mr. Nicholson watched with a smile. He gestured to the injury high on Bess's hip, and Jimmy put the back of his hand over his mouth, trying not to laugh.

Blake had finished examining Bess's high leg, straightened and found the sutures. "Oh," he said sheepishly.

"Will she live, Dr. Blake?" asked Jimmy in a false high pitched voice.

"Not if you're the owner," said Blake.

Mr. Nicholson laid a hand on the mare's withers. "She's all right. She's a tough old mare. She's thirty years old, you know."

Blake patted the mare's neck. "She's in great shape. How long have you had her?"

"All of her life. When she was born, I put my hands around her narrow baby ribs and helped her stand."

"Cool," Jimmy said, envious that horses live so much longer than dogs.

Blake asked, "How did Bess get hurt? She looked okay when we caught her."

"She was. But she was in such a snit that two boys had caught her, that she decided she didn't want to stay with me. She pulled back and hit a railing almost buried in the snow. After that, she was quite contrite," said Mr. Nicholson.

"How did you end up here?" Jimmy asked.

"Ah, now that's a story," said Mr. Nicholson. "A good friend of yours took me here." He glanced at Jimmy, smiling.

"A friend of mine?" Jimmy couldn't imagine who that would be.

"She's outside by my truck," said Mr. Nicholson. "She declined to come into the hospital."

Katie? But how? Jimmy couldn't imagine who else could have directed Mr. Nicholson here.

"Come on, Bess, love," said Mr. Nicholson. "Time for us to be off." Blake opened the stall door. Jimmy pushed open the large doors. Mr. Nicholson led the blanketed mare outside.

The hard, cold storm clouds brewed into rumpled, angry masses and the wind kicked up small snow flurries.

Jimmy walked down the length of pipe paddocks. Jimmy noticed Mr. Nicholson's '75 deep blue Ford full-sized pickup—*a classically cool truck,* he thought. It was parked nearby under a snow-silvered Eastern white pine.

Every year just before Christmas, Jimmy and Blake had tied chunks of bread to the tree, along with bunches of millet and suet, and smeared peanut butter on pine cones for the many hungry birds and squirrels. Jimmy realized he hadn't even thought about it this year. *Tomorrow* he told himself firmly. *We'll do it tomorrow.*

As Jimmy reached the side of the truck, no one was sitting in the cab. Jimmy started to ask, "Who?" when a familiar face appeared, peeking around the front end of the truck.

"Lassie!"

She charged toward him, jumping and barking in her usual friendly way.

Jimmy bent down on one knee and hugged her neck. "I should have known it was you. How did you get here?" he asked. She pulled back, barked at him, then barked toward Bess and Mr. Nicholson.

"Okay," Jimmy said. "You had to help Bess and Mr. Nicholson, didn't you?" She wagged her tail, licked his chin and trotted over to Bess. The Morgan mare lowered her dark head and sniffed the golden fur of the collie.

Jimmy smiled. *Another Lassie adventure*, Jimmy thought. A couple years ago Jimmy had taught Lassie how to unlatch the back door and gate. In case there was a fire and no one was home, he wanted her to be able to get herself out safely. So now she could come and go at will, although Jimmy had to admit she seemed to leave only when she was needed by someone. Today it had been Bess and Mr. Nicholson.

"Now how did you know he needed help?" Jimmy asked, rubbing her head. She barked again and bounded up to Blake who scratched her itchiest spot, the base between her ears.

"Okay, my friend," said Mr. Nicholson. "In you go." He let down the ramp of the horse trailer and Bess ambled inside. He leaned through the small window in the front of the trailer, secured the mare's lead line, then shut the ramp-tailgate.

This was all going too fast for Jimmy. He followed the old man around to the driver's side of the cab, Lassie at his heels. He wondered again at the red stenciled letters on the side of the truck cap. The horse in the drawing looked an awful lot like Bess.

"Is this Bess here?" Jimmy asked, pointing to the painted horse. He was stalling for time, trying to think how to ask politely if the old man had enough to eat, a place to stay. Maybe Mr. Nicholson was homeless.

Mr. Nicholson laughed. "Bess isn't that old! No, that's her great-granddam, though. It was my father's horse. Oh, how he loved the Morgan breed. The first American horse bred in the United States, you know. My father was very patriotic too."

Blake studied the drawing of a man and a horse-drawn wagon on the side of the truck topper. "You do this yourself?"

"Yes, I did, Master Blake. I tried to make it like an old photo I have of my father." Mr. Nicholson stepped to the driver's side of the pickup, opened the door, and took a photo down that had been stuck in the visor. He walked back to where the boys were standing and handed them the photo.

Blake grinned. "Nice work. It looks just like the picture."

"Thank you."

"Did your dad travel around in that wagon?" Jimmy asked.

"Yes," Mr. Nicholson replied. "Actually, I was pretty young when he died. I got most of the information about him from my mother. She would travel with my father when they were first married. Now that I'm retired, I like to travel around with ol' Bess here. It gives me a chance to help people when they need help. I'm not bound by having to be here or there."

"Sounds exciting," Blake replied.

Mr. Nicholson was full of surprises. Jimmy didn't want to just leave and never see him again. So he blurted out, "Where are you going?" Mr. Nicholson couldn't stay outside tonight, could he? "It's supposed to storm again tonight," Jimmy added lamely.

Mr. Nicholson paused, his calm eyes twinkling. "Why Jimmy, don't you worry. We're staying at your house."

4

The Grouchy Neighbor

Jimmy was first startled, then wary. What was this? An elaborate scheme? Was Mr. Nicholson some kind of homeless con artist?

Blake, seeing Jimmy's face, burst out laughing.

"What's so funny?" he growled. Lassie nuzzled his hand, whining.

"You look like you've just seen a ghost," Blake said, grinning.

"I don't believe in ghosts," snapped Jimmy.

"Easy, man," said Blake as an amused Mr. Nicholson watched. "Think how this might have happened. Come on, jock brain. Think."

Jimmy glared at him, embarrassed as well as angry. He felt like the only one not in on the joke. He didn't know how Mr. Nicholson could be invited to his house unless he had invited him.

Mr. Nicholson fixed his calm eyes on him. Lassie walked over to the old man, her tail waving. She was rarely wrong about strangers, knowing the good from the bad.

Lassie came back to Jimmy and he pulled her into his arms. "Lassie thinks you're a friend," he said. "I believe her. But how," he broke off, uncertain.

Jimmy looked up and noticed the fancy scrolls of faded gold paint on the side of the horse trailer. Among the lavish painted flowers were the fading letters: Toymaker and Mender.

"May I give you boys a ride home?" offered Mr. Nicholson. "I can explain my story on the way."

Blake shook his head. "I gotta clean those kennels."

Jimmy started to say he needed to help, but Blake interrupted him. "Nah, go with the man. I'll do this. You can help tomorrow. No problem."

Before Jimmy could protest, Blake had jogged back to the barn.

Mr. Nicholson slid onto the wide seat of his old truck. The bench seat's springs squeaked. He patted the seat cushion with his hand. "There's room for you and your fine dog," he called.

Jimmy went and grabbed his coat, then ran around to the other side of the cab and opened the door. Lassie easily sprang onto the seat with Jimmy clambering in beside her. Mr. Nicholson drew his hat down tighter on his head, put the truck in gear, and said, "Let's go."

The pickup jerked a little to start, then began rolling

smoothly out of the parking lot of the vet hospital and onto Second Street.

"Hang a right at the corner," instructed Jimmy.

They stayed to the far right. Bess neighed loudly, not knowing where Mr. Nicholson was headed. People in cars pulled up next to them and stared. Mr. Nicholson rolled down the window, waved happily, and called, "Merry Christmas!"

This is wild, was all Jimmy could think. "So how did you get to know Lassie?" he asked Mr. Nicholson.

The old man patted Lassie's head. "After you and Blake hurried off to school, I noticed Bess was bleeding. While I examined her wound, your lovely collie trotted up to me. She seemed to understand our situation, and she barked at me. Then she ran a few feet away and stopped and barked again. I got the idea that she wanted us to follow. So that's what we did. And she brought us to the animal hospital."

Jimmy marveled that a stranger would just follow an unknown dog because it seemed the thing to do.

"Take a left up there," said Jimmy, pointing at the next street. Cars and trucks whizzed by, their exhaust fumes white in the cold air.

"To make a long story short," said Mr. Nicholson, stopping at the red light. "At the animal hospital, a Dr. Smith happened to be there, and he offered to stitch her up. I'm sure we made him late to his appointment."

"That's Blake's dad," said Jimmy.

"The same," agreed Mr. Nicholson. "A gracious gentleman. Dr. Smith told me who Lassie was and gave me your father's number at church. I told the reverend how Lassie led me to the animal hospital for my injured horse."

"What did Dad say to that?" asked Jimmy, fascinated.

"He laughed and said that didn't surprise him one bit. So your father came down here to take Lassie home, we got to talking, and he found out about my being a toy mender. He invited me to help with the toy drive at your church. I agreed and then he invited me to stay with you folks."

"That sounds like Dad," said Jimmy knowingly. Dad was always inviting people to stay at their house. "How long will you be staying?"

"Oh probably until the toy drive is over," Mr. Nicholson replied.

This should be interesting, Jimmy thought. He smiled and said, "Turn up there—to the left. We can drive in through the back gate."

The sky had darkened with dusk and with the building storm. Snowflakes hit the windshield steadily and the noisy wiper blades squeaked as they cleared the flakes away. When they approached the Harmons' back gate, Jimmy jumped out and swung wide the gate, allowing Mr. Nicholson to drive through.

"Jimmy!" a voice rang out behind him. He turned, startled. Mr. Krebs, their next-door neighbor, stood with both hands on his hips, glaring. "I thought your family said there would be no more horses in your backyard."

Jimmy clutched the open gate. Mr. Krebs was the grumpiest neighbor in this area, probably in Farley, mostly likely on earth!

When Sarah was six, she was given a pony by a church member who was moving and couldn't take it along. The fuss Mr. Krebs made about a pony in the backyard! And their backyard was big, too—big enough to keep several horses. And Dad had made Sarah and Jimmy rake the corral and shed every day. No way did it smell as bad as Mr. Krebs claimed.

A year later the pony was sold because Sarah hadn't been interested any more in taking care of it. Then it was Jimmy's turn for a pet, and he was given a puppy—Lassie. The complaints continued. "Lassie barked all night long."

Never. Lassie never did that. But you couldn't convince Mr. Krebs of anything.

"The horse is here for just a few nights," said Jimmy, hating the way his voice stretched out, nervous as an unearthed earthworm. "Mr. Nicholson is here to help us with the church toy drive."

Mr. Krebs didn't care much about anything related to church. He looked about ready to blast his opinion about church when Mr. Nicholson appeared at Jimmy's shoulder.

"Is there a problem, sir?" he asked politely, fixing his eyes on Mr. Krebs.

For a moment Jimmy thought his neighbor was going to flash into one of his famous tirades, but he just said gruffly, "Don't want to listen to a horse whinnying its head off."

"Oh, Bess will be quiet, I assure you," said Mr. Nicholson. "And I'm merely here for a couple of days."

Snow was beginning to swirl down, collecting on Lassie's back. She had run up behind Mr. Nicholson and was leaning against Jimmy's leg. Suddenly she gave a happy yip and pranced past Mr. Krebs to Mr. Krebs's grand-daughter, Megan. She was seven years old, and lived with Mr. and Mrs. Krebs.

Jimmy always thought, *Poor kid, to have to live with Mr. Krebs.*

Megan flung her arms around Lassie's neck.

Mr. Krebs shouted, "Leave that dog alone, Margaret!"

Megan jumped back guiltily, and Mr. Krebs hurried her back to his house.

"I'm so glad you got to meet our wonderful neighbor," said Jimmy.

To his surprise Mr. Nicholson only said, "I've met a lot of Mr. Krebses in my life. They don't bother me."

Well, he sure bothers me, thought Jimmy as they hurried to put Bess in the shed. Anyone who doesn't love animals, especially a pet like Lassie, must be a miserable person.

Jimmy helped Mr. Nicholson toss some hay to the mare and filled an old washtub with water. Mr. Nicholson buckled Bess's blanket over her back, then Jimmy showed him to the back door of the house.

"We're home!" called Jimmy as they slipped into the warmth of the house.

"Come on in," Mr. Harmon said, walking into the kitchen with the daily newspaper still in his hands. "We've been waiting for you two to get here."

5

What, Another Dog?

Saturday morning Mr. Nicholson went with Dad to the church. He'd taken an old, carved wooden chest full of tools and toy supplies with him, but he'd left Bess to rest and heal in the shed with a pile of hay to munch. Sarah and Jimmy visited Bess while Mom was making breakfast, and they fed her a bag of carrots.

After breakfast Jimmy filled his backpack with a loaf of bread and a jar of peanut butter. He told his Mom, "I'm going to the animal hospital." He'd buy millet and suet at the pet store on his way.

"Don't forget about rehearsal," reminded his mom. "One o'clock sharp."

Jimmy rolled his eyes. "You know, I'm getting too old to do the pageant, Mom. I feel stupid with all those kindergarten angels and shepherds with runny noses."

"I know how to make Jimmy want to be in the pageant, Mom," said Sarah. "Spice it up a little. Throw in some sex appeal and have Joseph kiss Mary. Jimmy will totally be

39

happy to be in the pageant."

"Sarah!" Mom exclaimed. "For heaven's sake!"

"Shut up," Jimmy snapped. He played Joseph this year and Katie Madison was Mary. Sex appeal in the Christmas pageant! He laughed, but his ears turned red as he thought about kissing Katie. He and Katie had been friends for a long time. No, they were more than good friends; at least Jimmy thought so. Lassie barked as Sarah snickered.

"Just be there at one, James Harmon," said Mom.

He sighed. "Don't worry, Mom. I will." Sometimes he wished he was just totally rebellious and out of control. Instead of going to the pageant rehearsal he would—what? Hot-wire a car and drive one hundred twenty miles an hour to some wild theme park? He laughed at himself. Hot-wire a car. Like he could. With his luck it would be a stick shift, and he'd kill the engine and get arrested before he got down the block.

He called for Lassie and they went out the door. Sarah was making kissing noises behind him. Sometimes he wished he was an only child.

Lassie trotted alongside Jimmy as he jogged down the newly plowed road. Sometimes Jimmy would slide on an icy patch, pretending to be a great Olympic skater. Lassie would get excited, jump and bark as Jimmy flailed his arms this way and that.

"Hey, what's the matter, girl?" Jimmy said teasingly.

"Don't you like my style, my perfect form? Definitely six point 0." They jogged on.

Jimmy let himself into the animal hospital through the staff entrance in the back. Lassie clicked after him, totally at home. They hurried down the corridor leading from the hospital to the kennels.

Blake was petting a half-grown, wildly-furred puppy who was as big as Lassie. "Hey, Jim." He let the puppy bound up to Lassie.

"That's not a puppy; that's a small monster," said Jimmy as the puppy leaped up on him. The pup looked like a cross between a Great Dane and a standard poodle. It was huge pawed with curly tufts of fur all over its body.

"Maybe we could send him to the local auction disguised as a sheep," said Blake. "He might get a home that way."

Lassie sniffed the gangly puppy gently, then gave a playful bark and they were off, tearing down the cement aisle, Lassie chasing. The other dogs barked encouragement and longing.

"How long has he been here?" asked Jimmy.

"Just about a month," said Blake. "If he'd been at the county shelter, he'd been put to sleep by now."

An awful thought. Jimmy sighed. "He'd be a great dog for some kid, wouldn't he?" said Jimmy. "He'd make a great Christmas gift."

Blake grinned. "Why not give him to that little girl?"

"What little girl?"

"You know, the little kid next door to you."

Jimmy guffawed. "Mr. Krebs would have heart failure."

"That's the point!"

They both cracked up.

While Lassie exercised the big puppy up and down the two aisles, the penned dogs barked madly. Jimmy helped Blake hose down the cement runs of each inmate as Dr. Smith called them, his ears ringing from the noise.

Sometimes owners came to the hospital with pets they wanted put to sleep just because they were tired of caring for that dog or cat. The vets generally convinced the owner to put an ad in the paper to give the animal to someone else or, if all else failed, they offered to keep the animal and put it up for adoption.

Today all ten dog runs were full. In fact, two runs had doubled up with dogs. The small cattery, stacks of wire cat cages off to one side, were all full too.

"This one looks purebred," said Jimmy, peering at a Siamese which meowed in its harsh yowl.

"Probably is," said Blake, reaching a hand through the wire. The cat rubbed its chocolate head against his fingers. "This one got hit by a car. A stranger brought it in and Dr. Holson had to pin his hip and take out his spleen."

"Yuck," said Jimmy, but he marveled that the cat had

survived and was now beautifully restored.

After they cleaned the cats' litter boxes and returned the big puppy to his run, Jimmy, Blake, and Lassie went out to hang food from the pine they had named "the animals' Christmas tree."

"Dr. Davies helped me string lights this morning," said Blake, pointing at the pine. The top of the tree was more than eight feet high, but perched up there was a dog and cat angel, holding paws, mouths open singing praises. The tree's boughs dripped tiny, colored lights, softly gleaming in the gray day.

"Cool," said Jimmy.

For the next hour, they tied bread, sprigs of millet, and suet on branches for the birds. Around the base of the tree, they ladled cat food. When they were finishing up, a shrill woman's voice called, "You boys wouldn't want a dog, would you?"

Mutant Dust Ball

The dog, if you could call it that, was no more than ten inches high with stiff, tan fur springing out in all directions. For a moment, Jimmy could tell only where its head was because the leash came from one general direction.

The dog, however, had no clue he was small. He pranced as far as his leash allowed to investigate Lassie, unafraid, bold, yapping like a wind-up toy. Genteelly Lassie lowered her muzzle and sniffed the tiny canine. He strained to get even closer, rearing on his short hind legs, his front feet swimming. The tiny dog began hacking, but didn't pull on the leash.

"Bandy, if you would just settle down," said the woman.

Jimmy cleared his throat and put on his best church usher look, asking, "Have you tried the hospital shelter?"

"I just did. It's full," said the woman. "I can't take him back home. We're moving to an apartment with no animals allowed."

"That's not an animal," hissed Blake, as he bent over the

45

furry, choking thing. "It's a mutant dust ball."

Jimmy covered a laugh with a cough. The woman gazed at them anxiously. "Please, can't you take him? If I go back with him, my husband will drown him. He really will. See, your dog likes him already."

Bandy jumped at Lassie, front legs flailing, still gasping and yapping in turns. Lassie looked bemused as if she wasn't sure if she ought to humor this miniature dog or not. Once when Lassie was about a year old, Jimmy and his family had visited Grandpa and Grandma Harmon in Florida. They had an apricot-colored teacup poodle named Max. Lassie and Max had come inside from roaming in the yard. Lassie had sat down. And suddenly Max started yapping wildly. Lassie began searching for Max, unable to see him. Where was he? Max kept barking, quite close by.

Lassie had been sitting on Max! Only his head poked out from under her long fur, and he barked like a squashed cartoon. Jimmy and Sarah had laughed their heads off for days over the flattened Max.

Jimmy thought fast about Bandy. Surely someone would want a little dog. Perhaps an elderly woman from church would want a companion. Then she wouldn't have to deal with the nonsense of a puppy, all the chewing, teething, barking, housebreaking. Jimmy bet he could talk one of the older women into taking the dog. There was Mrs. Chase who used to have a sheltie until last year when the dog had died. Maybe Mrs. Ramos. She had a tank of tropical fish and four zebra finches. She liked animals.

"Okay, I'll take him," Jimmy said.

"Jimmy!" Blake stood straight up. "The shelter is full. There's nowhere to put him."

"I think I know somebody who'll want him. He'll be a Christmas present," said Jimmy, suddenly inspired. "Yeah, a Christmas present." To whom he would give the dog he had no clue, but surely he could find a house for one little dog. Couldn't he?

"Oh, thank you, thank you. Bless you. Thank you." The woman actually began to cry. Jimmy was embarrassed. But before he could respond, the woman merely shoved the end of the leash into his hand and bolted for her car parked on the street.

Bandy, the leash suddenly loosened, fell forward with a shocked yelp. But he instantly bounced back up like a bouncing rubber ball. He went ballistic between Jimmy, Blake, and Lassie, jumping back and forth like an electron. He didn't even seem to notice his mistress had gone.

"Is this dog on speed, or what?" asked Blake.

"Really. He needs Doggie Downers," said Jimmy. "Bandy, sit." Bandy acted as if he hadn't even heard Jimmy. Lassie sat gracefully as if to give him the idea, but the dog merely launched an attack on her tail.

"Bandy, sit," insisted Jimmy.

Bandy never even looked at him.

Blake shrugged. "Maybe he doesn't speak English?"

Jimmy pushed on the dog's skinny haunches, but Bandy merely wheeled around and playfully attacked his hand. Oh, well. So much for dog training.

"Now what?" asked Blake as Bandy rolled on his back in the snow, kicking all four legs at Lassie's belly.

Jimmy looked at his watch. "Now we go to church rehearsal."

"With him?" Blake pointed at the supercharged canine. "What can I do with him?"

"Your mom is gonna kill you," said Blake cheerfully.

She'll kill me and then kill me again, Jimmy thought and sighed. Why did his good deeds seem to cause so much trouble?

7

In the Doghouse

The four of them, two boys and two dogs, slipped into church through the side door of the kitchen. The clock on the wall read one seventeen.

Lassie trotted on into the church sanctuary through the swinging kitchen doors without hesitation. What should they do about Bandy? Jimmy and Blake exchanged looks. Jimmy wanted to explain to Mom but not in front of all the kids from the pageant. It was going to be tricky enough without an audience. So what could he do with the little dog?

"Jimmy!" Mom's voice, strained and impatient, filled the air as she came toward the kitchen, Lassie's entrance having tipped her off that Jimmy was now here. By her tone of voice, he knew he was already in deep trouble.

Quickly he opened one of the lower cupboard doors. Cast-iron pots and pans rested in neat rows. Jimmy reached in and shoved the pans to the side, then grabbed the startled Bandy and jammed him inside, tossing his leash after him before he shut the door. Jimmy spied an open box of

49

crackers, opened the cupboard again, dumped a pile of crackers into a pan, then shut the cupboard door, making sure to latch it.

"Come on," Jimmy demanded to Blake who was laughing. Jimmy grabbed his buddy's arm and hauled him out into the main part of the church.

Mom gave him a look that said, "When I get you home you are in big trouble."

Jimmy tried to return a look that said, "I can explain," but Mom wasn't trying to understand.

"Jimmy, on the stage with Katie. Blake, over there with the other two wise men," Mrs. Harmon directed. Every year Mom coordinated the Christmas pageant. Personally Jimmy thought she ought to give it a rest, but hey, no one asked for his advice.

He stood next to Katie by the cardboard prop cradle. The real cradle was brought out only for the performance. The baby Jesus was a red superhero doll—not exactly an appropriate substitute. Katie smiled at him.

"Jesus probably would have made a good superhero," whispered Jimmy.

Katie giggled. "It was all we could find in the nursery, except a stuffed elephant."

"Given those two choices, the superhero is definitely the better choice," said Jimmy.

"Joseph and Mary, quiet!" said Mom. She nodded to

Wanda Bradley, a skinny sixth grader, sitting demurely on the piano bench, her lanky hair in a ponytail. Wanda banged the keys, rocketing into "Angels We Have Heard on High."

Lassie peeked around the edge of the first pew bench. Jimmy wondered if she was going to sing along—she had a great howl. But she stood quietly, alert as if she was the drama critic. The angels stumbled through their song and Jimmy felt like howling. How could Wanda butcher that song? After about ten minutes, Lassie turned and left. Jimmy hardly blamed her.

"Shepherds, your cue," Mrs. Harmon called, as a cluster of first graders wobbled up the main aisle, pretending to wave shepherds' crooks.

"Lethal weapons," whispered Jimmy. "They'd put out their sheep's eyes if they really had shepherds' crooks."

Katie giggled. Then after a moment she whispered, "What is that noise?"

Jimmy didn't hear anything at first except Wanda hitting wrong notes during "O Little Town of Bethlehem." He and Katie were to sing a song together to Wanda's playing. That was a depressing thought. The girl needed major help.

"There," said Katie, bumping his arm with her elbow. "Hear it?"

A low wavering tone rose up above the tinny piano notes. Jimmy froze, knowing exactly what it was.

"Hear it?" Katie asked. It grew louder, shriller, then sharply broke off. A huge crashing like giant cymbals burst from the kitchen.

He heard it all right. But he replied, "I don't hear anything."

An unsteady silence crossed through the church. Kids stared at each other. Wanda gallantly continued playing.

Katie looked at Jimmy as if he'd sprouted another head. "Are you deaf?"

"After hearing Wanda play, I wish I were," he muttered.

The shepherds paused at the bottom of the steps to the platform and altar, where the baby Jesus, alias the red superhero, lay. They glanced around nervously as if they feared a pack of wolves was about to attack their imaginary sheep.

"Is that Robby McAllister?" demanded Mom. "Where is he?" Robby was the notorious fourth-grade Sunday school prankster.

"Right here, Mrs. Harmon," called Robby. He waved from a pack of kids playing the inn dwellers. "It wasn't me. Honest."

The howl began again, swelling, brimming with edged notes that ripped at one's ears. Katie put her hands over her ears. "What a horrible noise," she said. Jimmy just wanted to disappear.

"Something is dying," declared one of the shepherds.

Jimmy knew someone would die soon—him.

Mom studied her nativity scene with a probing, knowing look. Jimmy squirmed, clenching and unclenching his fingers, imploring Bandy to shut up, go to sleep, have a stroke, anything.

Suddenly Bandy quieted.

Thank you, God, thought Jimmy.

Lassie, bored with the rehearsal, had shoved open the swinging kitchen door with her head. She smelled the little dog, but couldn't see him. But a munching sound came from one of the cupboards. She cocked her head, puzzled, and scratched at the cupboard. The munching stopped, a little growl rumbled out, then more munching. She scratched at the cupboard again. More growls. So she laid down, waiting until the munching stopped.

About fifteen minutes later, Bandy had eaten the pile of stale crackers. Now he wanted out of this dark place. He hurled himself against the shut door. Lassie stood and scratched at the door again. He began to yowl. She jiggled the latch but was unable to open it. Bandy howled louder.

She needed to get help. She knew better than to interrupt Mrs. Harmon, so she trotted outside to the education building where the toy mending and food sorting for the Christmas baskets was going on.

She found Mr. Nicholson and put her paw on his knee. She whined and moved away. "You want me to follow you again, my lass?" asked Mr. Nicholson. He politely excused himself from the other workers and followed Lassie once more.

More cymbal crashing burst from the kitchen. Wanda clashed chords and complained, "I can't concentrate with that racket going on."

"She said it," darkly muttered an angel. "Her music is racket."

Giggles rose up from the inn folks and spread to the angels. Soon the little shepherds were cracking up, without quite knowing why.

Mary had to sit down next to her baby superhero because she was laughing so hard. Only Jimmy and Mrs. Harmon weren't laughing.

Mom turned her dark gaze on Jimmy now. "James Stephen Harmon," she began, when the kitchen door popped opened. Mr. Nicholson stepped through, holding a hysterical Bandy with Lassie at his heels.

I'm in the doghouse this time, thought Jimmy, wishing he could hide in the kitchen cupboard.

8

Weird as Life

"**H**e was in the kitchen cupboard," declared Mr. Nicholson. "Isn't that something?"

A couple of shepherds ran over to pet the wriggling Bandy. Maybe Jimmy could pretend he had no clue. He could say with a puzzled look, "A dog in the cupboard? I have no idea how it got there."

"Jimmy!" Mom roared.

He decided playing dumb probably was not going to work. Reluctantly he dragged across the makeshift stable and dropped down the stairs. "I can explain, Mom," he started.

"If this is your idea of a joke, it's not funny," hissed Mrs. Harmon, gripping his elbow so tight he thought she'd pop the joint. Mom might've been slender, but she was strong.

"No, see there was this lady," said Jimmy, breaking off to try to squirm free.

"Stand still while you're talking to me, young man."

"Mom! You're breaking my arm!"

Mr. Nicholson came over, his calm eyes fixed on Mom. "If I may interrupt, Mrs. Harmon. I can watch over this wee beastie and keep him quiet until your practice is over."

Mom let go. Jimmy backed up just in case she decided to stick out her arm again.

A change seemed to come over Mom. She blinked, then said, "Thank you, Mr. Nicholson. That would be very kind." Turning from Jimmy, she clapped her hands. "Children! Children! Places! We'll start in again right after the angels have sung 'Hark, the Herald.'"

Jimmy gave Mr. Nicholson a relieved and thankful smile. He hurried back to his place by the infant and Katie Madison, alias Mary.

The rest of the rehearsal was uneventful; in fact, boring. Jimmy had been through this pageant, how many times? He thought a moment. Dad's been pastor here since I was in first grade. So this was the seventh time. Seven times! The same old, same old. This was his second time being Joseph. Major boredom.

No offense, God, but old Joe wasn't too exciting, Jimmy thought to himself. He just kind of was there at the right time. Poor dude.

"Jimmy," said Mom. She sounded as if she'd said it more than once in the last twenty seconds.

Katie punched his ribs. "Our song," she hissed and they moved away from the cardboard box acting as a cradle to the mikes on the edge of the platform.

Wanda dropped a sheaf of music and was hunting for pages under the piano. Jimmy shifted his weight. Lassie had curled up on the floor in front of the first pew and had gone to sleep. Not that he didn't blame her.

Wanda sat back down, straightened pages, then arching her hands over the keys, she charged into the music.

"Slowly," commanded Mom. "This is a thoughtful song."

That much was right. Jimmy still couldn't believe that last year he'd written the music. And Katie had written the words. The melody was haunting and quieted the children.

Jimmy and Katie sang:

"We are travelers alone in this world.

If it wasn't for God, we'd lose our way.

Even now, we wonder, *Are we on the right path*?

A strange city, a cold night, with only a bed of hay?"

Then Katie stepped forward and sang in her clear, strong, alto voice:

"Barely a child, You have asked much of me.

The night is empty of warmth and friends,

No one understands how this is for me,

Only we and the animals to welcome the newborn king."

Then Jimmy came forward as Katie stepped back. His stomach always got jittery when he stood alone in front of people to perform. Lassie opened her eyes and lifted her head as he began to sing his own part. Then together, he and Katie finished the pondering, slow song, the last notes dwindling like stretched taffy, sweet and warm.

"Gotta slow down, Wanda," Mom said, shaking her head. "Still too fast."

Finally they finished practicing at four. Long, evening shadows unfurled their dark selves into the church sanctuary. Counterbalancing the dark, muted light tumbled in through the vertical stained-glass windows in shining puddles of colors on the pews and floor.

"Boys and girls," called Mom as kids jumped from the platform and began pulling on jackets and mittens. "Dress rehearsal Wednesday. One o'clock sharp!" She glared at Jimmy as she said it.

Sheesh, as if he was the only late one. Four kids had come in after him. Being a preacher's kid was not all it was cracked up to be.

"Hear that?" Jimmy demanded, grabbing the red superhero and shaking him. "You gotta look like a baby by Wednesday."

"You are so weird, Jimmy Harmon," declared Katie, zipping her parka.

"Thank you," Jimmy said bowing low as if he had just performed a piece written by a great composer.

Blake yelled on his way out, "Good luck!" Jimmy groaned. Maybe he was coming down with a serious disease.

Katie turned to Jimmy. "What did Blake mean?"

So Jimmy told her about the lady and how she left Bandy with them. Katie listened without talking, unlike most girls who always had to jump in with smart comments or dumb questions that had nothing to do with anything. That was another reason he liked being with Katie.

When he was done, she said thoughtfully, "You know, my Great-Aunt Elizabeth lives alone. I wonder if she'd want Bandy." Katie zipped and unzipped her parka, thinking. Then she pulled the zipper tag to her chin and said, "I'll take Bandy. I think Aunt Elizabeth would like having a small dog. She likes Rags when we visit. It'll help me because I never know what to give her."

"Sure," said Jimmy, amazed it was so easy to rid himself of the dog. "Thanks," he added, his heart lifting.

"I'll go get Bandy from Mr. Nicholson." She ran off and left him wondering how she knew Mr. Nicholson since he'd only met the old man yesterday.

Life was weird, he reminded himself and whistled for Lassie to head home.

9

Animal Friends

That evening it was Jimmy's turn to do the dishes. When he was finished, he popped in a Christian rock CD and stretched out in front of the fire in the fireplace with Lassie alongside him. Mom was in the bedroom, the door tightly shut, having issued stern warnings that no one, but NO ONE, was allowed admittance.

Dad had a deacons' meeting at seven at the church. Sarah was in her room doing who knows what. She said she was wrapping presents, but Jimmy saw her drag the extension phone into her room. Probably yacking to one of her friends. They could talk for hours! What was going to happen when she became a teenager? Surgically have the phone attached to her ear?

In five days Jimmy would be a teenager. The big count-down had begun. He wondered if he would feel any different. Still, no one had said one word about his birthday. *Maybe they really have forgotten,* he thought. He wondered if he should drop a hint, but something stubborn in him said no way. Your family is supposed to remember your birthday. And if they forget, well, just pretend it was no big deal. When they finally remember, they'll be so sorry.

But he still wished someone would remember.

Mr. Nicholson sat in a chair at a card table. Jimmy watched him repair a toy engine, boxcar, and caboose, gluing little parts here and there and digging through a box for just the right wheel size.

"How did you become a toy mender?" asked Jimmy.

Mr. Nicholson glanced up and smiled, his eyes always seemed calm and quiet like moonlight glowing over sea water. "I like making children happy," he said. "This is a way I can do that."

"But do many people ask you to fix toys these days?" Jimmy rolled onto his stomach, propping his chin up with his fist.

"Not really," said Mr. Nicholson. He rolled the three-car train back and forth on its new wheels. "I've done work with antique toys, rocking horses, wooden toys, and dolls. I've restored some pieces for various museums."

"That's cool," said Jimmy. "So do you drive your old truck and horse trailer wherever you go?"

Mr. Nicholson's smile widened. "I do."

"Isn't that sort of hard?"

"I try to avoid the major streets if I can. Once I did some work for the Smithsonian. Things did get rather complex.

You can't just leave a horse in a trailer all day alone. But it all worked out okay."

Jimmy laughed to think of Mr. Nicholson driving that old pick-up and horse trailer down the major streets of Washington D.C.. Jimmy envisioned Nicholson's Traveling Show, just like in old movies. Jimmy thought it was totally cool that Mr. Nicholson was so different, not really caring what others thought of him.

Jimmy asked, "Why are people so weird about animals? Like they don't want you to bring your dog into a store."

Mr. Nicholson carefully wrapped the mended train in white tissue paper and placed it in a long, narrow box to be wrapped later. He picked up a clean, dry paintbrush and tapped it thoughtfully on the table. "Maybe people are threatened by animals," he said finally.

Jimmy wasn't sure he understood. "What do you mean?"

"Take your next-door neighbor, for instance."

You take him! thought Jimmy. But he asked, "What about him? He hates horses and dogs. He probably hates all animals. And it's not that he's scared of them."

"You might be surprised. It might be a deep fear of the unknown. After all, animals are their own selves. They basically behave the way they want. Some of them, like Lassie and my Bess, have willingly allied themselves with people. But even so, doesn't Lassie do things on her own, without you giving a command?"

Lassie lifted her head at her name, glancing from Mr. Nicholson to Jimmy.

"She sure does," said Jimmy. "Like going to see you the other morning."

"There you are," said Mr. Nicholson. "Some people are threatened by that willfulness."

"But she was doing something good," said Jimmy.

"Maybe people like Mr. Krebs realize they don't always do good things, but here a supposedly dumb animal does. What does that say about him?"

Jimmy wasn't sure. It seemed kind of confusing, but in a weird way it made sense, too. "Maybe you're right," he said, sitting up and stroking Lassie. The firelight enriched her coat so she shone bronze and gold like a metal sculpture.

Too bad more people didn't have animal friends, thought Jimmy. Maybe they'd be better people for it.

Jimmy hoped Katie's great-aunt would take Bandy. The dog was little but packed with personality. *Just another aspect of God's creativity,* he thought. God made so many kinds of animals. *Why? For fun? I bet to please people,* he thought. And sometimes people almost slap God in the face by rejecting and mistreating His animals!

An idea flashed into Jimmy's mind. He sat bolt upright and said suddenly, "I just had the best idea!"

Mr. Nicholson, sewing a stuffed lamb with a split seam down its belly, paused, a twinkle in his eye.

Jimmy said, "To get people to adopt the shelter animals for Christmas presents, we could do something at the mall —you know, set up a booth, have animals there all brushed and clean. People would see them and take them home for presents for their kids."

His mind brimmed with ideas of making flyers, posters, calling someone in charge of the mall, grooming the dogs and cats, tying bows and bells around their necks. "I bet the vets would help us too," Jimmy added. "Maybe offer a coupon for discount care with an adopted animal."

Mr. Nicholson said while continuing to sew the lamb's belly, "Good idea, Jimmy. Everyone will be happy with that. The pets, the owners, even the animal shelter."

Jimmy sat stroking Lassie's fur, his thoughts aglow about how everything would work. He'd start tomorrow, right after church. Christmas Pet Adoption Center—what an idea!

10

Megan

After church Jimmy, Blake, and Lassie—for she was definitely a partner in this venture—walked to the animal hospital. On the way they stopped for burgers (Lassie had a plain cheeseburger, hold the onions), french fries, and chocolate shakes. Jimmy figured shakes were better for you than soft drinks because at least you were getting some calcium. Right?

"Except some places serve nondairy shakes," said Blake.

Jimmy stared down into his cup at the last inch of chocolate shake as they walked along the sidewalk. *How could a milk shake be made with phony milk?* he thought to himself. "I hope it's not this place," he said.

Blake laughed. "Nothing is real anymore, is it?"

Jimmy thought about that and said, "Lassie is real. And so is Mr. Nicholson."

Blake agreed and counted on his fingers, "Lassie is real. Mr. Nicholson, include Bess in that, is real. Jesus is real. That's about it, isn't it?"

"Most of the time Jesus is real," said Jimmy. "But sometimes—doesn't it?—feel like He's a million miles away?"

"Yeah. But I think that's because we're standing in His shadow," said Blake.

Jimmy stared. "What do you mean?"

"My dad told me," he said, "that it's like when he's vetting a horse or a cow. They're such big animals that sometimes he forgets about the whole horse or cow and thinks about only one part that's sick. That's when he tells himself he's just standing in the horse's shadow and he needs to move back to see the whole horse again."

Jimmy thought about it some more. "I like that," he said. "I think I understand it."

Blake grinned. "I know. I like it too. So now you can explain it to me!"

At the animal shelter they sat down near the work station, Blake pulling out a notebook. "First things first," said Blake. "What to do. I'll take notes."

"Adopt out all the pets," said Jimmy. "That's the goal." Blake wrote it down.

"How do we do that?" asked Blake, chewing on the pen cap.

"Make flyers advertising the shelter and offering a pet for a Christmas present."

Blake wrote fast.

"We could put the flyers up at the mall, at a few grocery

stores, even the public library on the public events board."

Blake nodded and continued writing.

"We need to ask your dad about coupons for people who do take a pet," said Jimmy. "You know, maybe he could give a free exam visit or some flea powder or something with each pet."

They looked at each other for a while.

Jimmy said, "I still think we ought to go somewhere, like the mall, so people can see the dogs and cats."

Blake wrote and added, "We'll need to groom them, maybe wash the dogs, and have kids help hold the dogs and the cats.

"I'm sure Katie and some of the others will help," said Jimmy. He snapped his fingers. "I know! Let's ask Mr. Nicholson if he can help us. Maybe we could put a big sign on his truck and maybe transport the animals in the back. Then wherever he drives we'll get some free advertising. I wish I'd thought of it last night when I was talking to him. That will get people's attention!"

"Cool," said Blake. "I like it. So what's first?"

Jimmy stroked Lassie. "I'll talk to Mr. Nicholson tonight at home. I bet he'll help us. He was all for this idea last night. Let's make a list of kids to call for help and divide the list between you and me to call tonight, okay? We can sketch out a flyer idea, too."

They thought of twenty-one friends to ask to help with

grooming and handling. "Maybe some of them will want a Christmas pet," suggested Blake.

The rest of the afternoon, after cleaning the kennels and the cattery, they worked on the flyer.

After what seemed like twenty versions of the same information, Jimmy and Blake decided that they had a flyer that pleased them both. They ran down to church and used the copy machine in Dad's office to print fifty flyers. Jimmy also borrowed a box of thumbtacks. He left a note so Dad's secretary would know what they'd used.

He and Blake split the pile and stuck flyers around town, mostly at stores where people were Christmas shopping already.

It was dark when Jimmy and Lassie got home. He went in the back way to check on Bess. She was eating quietly in the darkness of the shed.

A small voice said, "Hi, Jimmy."

Jimmy jumped. Megan, Mr. Krebs's granddaughter, sat on a hay bale.

"Hi, Megan," he said, glancing around to be sure Mr. Krebs wasn't lurking somewhere.

"Don't worry," said Megan. "Grandpa's in the house. He thinks I'm just taking out the trash."

Jimmy laughed uneasily. "Is it hard to live with him?"

Megan shook her pink-capped head. "It was worse with my mom and stepdad."

"Oh." Jimmy didn't know what to say to that except living with them must have really been awful. He didn't think he wanted to know the details.

"Grandpa's okay," Megan continued. "But I wish he'd let me have a dog like Lassie. Or a kitten."

"Yeah," said Jimmy. "I know what you mean." It was sad to think of the homeless animals in the shelter and Megan, who would be a perfect owner for one of them.

"I'll tell you what," said Jimmy. "You can be Lassie's adopted owner, okay?"

Megan smiled. "What does that mean?"

"Well," Jimmy said, making it up fast. "When you see Lassie, you can act like she's yours, too. You can pet her and give her treats. If your grandfather doesn't mind, you can walk her too."

"I don't think he'd allow me to do that," she said. "He doesn't like dogs. But maybe when I'm taking out the trash or something, I can come and see her."

"Sure," said Jimmy. "Anytime."

"Thanks," she said and got up to leave. "I'd better get back." She hugged the collie, then ran off into the night.

Jimmy and Lassie went into their house. Jimmy wondered if life ever grew fair for some people.

Assembly-Line Grooming

Five kids, including Katie with her lively dog, Rags, showed up Monday morning at ten o'clock at the animal shelter.

"Mr. Nicholson said we can use his pickup!" yelled Jimmy. He and Blake high-fived and whooped. The others hadn't seen the classic old truck, but Jimmy was sure they'd think it was awesome.

"So what do we do?" asked Alexander, a tall, blond kid. He held a plastic bucket with a dog brush, a leash, and a bottle of dog shampoo.

"This morning we're gonna wash and groom the dogs in the heated garage area in the back of the shelter. We'll just brush the cats," said Jimmy. He and Blake had talked with Dr. Smith about what was best to do and that had been his advice.

Everyone moved to the heated garage and set up an assembly line. Two kids began soaping up a black cocker spaniel with badly snarled fur at the wash station. The dog yelped a few times, but then settled down, enjoying the attention, even if he was wet. Then two more kids, Alexander and Lindsey, began washing a retriever mix.

Next to the wash area was a heavy-duty dryer. Katie turned it on and blasted Jimmy with hot air. "It works," she announced.

He yelped, sounding like the wet dog.

Another girl, Melissa, with wide, blue eyes and long, straight brown hair, helped Katie begin to dry the cocker spaniel, rubbing him with towels, fluffing his silky, wavy fur. Then when he was dry, they tied bows in his fur on both ears.

"He's so cute," exclaimed Katie.

Meanwhile washers had started in on a half-grown dalmatian-and-chow mix. Blake and another guy, Kevin, began combing the cats.

Jimmy sat on the floor with his notebook, figuring they could hit the shopping strip on First Street. Maybe go to the boutique shop over on Elm, then if they had animals left, and he hoped they didn't, they could go on over to the Old West Shoppe—the feed and tack store. Mr. Nicholson promised to drive over to the animal hospital at one o'clock sharp.

Lassie supervised the baths. If a particular dog seemed especially alarmed, she would walk over and lower her muzzle to the scared canine, seeming to reassure the animal. Even the cats seemed to appreciate her presence. One Siamese purred loudly each time she appeared. Mostly she stayed by the dogs, occasionally playing with her friend Rags and when they brought out the big puppy, she chased him around the garage.

Four dogs were clean and dry by eleven. The remaining dogs barked jealously in their kennels. The girls went all out decorating the dogs. Red, green, silver, and gold ribbons waved from ears. Collars with bells and sprigs of evergreen were around every clean neck, except one. The huge half-grown puppy kept eating his sprig. He even swallowed a bell. Katie ran for one of the vets on duty and he checked the puppy and said to look for the bell in his stool in the next day or so.

"Gross," exclaimed Katie. But at least the puppy was unhurt.

A little after twelve, when they had washed and dried all twelve dogs and brushed all eight cats, some of the vet workers brought in pizzas and soft drinks.

Jimmy hadn't even thought about lunch for his friends. Duh. Some leader. He thanked Anne, one of the health technicians (like an RN for animals). She was a knockout blonde, too.

"Thank you," Anne said. "You kids are doing a great thing. We wish we had time to do what you're doing, but we just don't. The patients take up all our time." She gave him a dazzling smile and said, "Merry Christmas!" Jimmy's knees nearly buckled, but he managed to say back, "Merry Christmas to you, too." He felt like saying, I'll wash dogs for you for the rest of my life, if you want. An age difference between us? Only a few years. Of course, I'm mature for almost thirteen. He laughed at himself. Dream on.

At one o'clock sharp Lassie barked at the outside shelter doors. When Jimmy threw them wide, Mr. Nicholson stood, arms outstretched, his face alight with joy.

"Look at you beauties!" he exclaimed. Jimmy wasn't sure if he meant the clean animals or the girls. Maybe both!

They carried the cats in cages to the back of the truck. Mr. Nicholson had taken out any loose junk from the back to make room for the cages and the kids.

"Dogs can ride inside the back of the truck with their handlers," said Mr. Nicholson. "We'll stack the cat cages up against the front of the long bed. When we reach the shopping strip, everyone can get out with the animals so people can see them better."

Everybody took a clean, leashed dog and scrambled into the pickup. Jimmy and Katie had two dogs each—their own, plus a shelter dog. Katie climbed into the back with the others, but Jimmy, Lassie, Mr. Nicholson, and the black cocker spaniel sporting red ribbons on his ears, sat on the bench seat of the truck.

Mr. Nicholson turned on the ignition and drove out of

the animal hospital parking lot.

"This is so cool," said Jimmy. "I just know every animal is going to find a home today."

"One already has," said Mr. Nicholson with a wink.

Jimmy gave him a puzzled look. "What do you mean?"

Mr. Nicholson jerked his chin at the black cocker spaniel. "Him and me." The dog was loving sitting on the bench. You could just tell. He sat unafraid as if he'd ridden on front seats all his life. His eyes were alert and he had one front paw on Mr. Nicholson's leg.

"Are you serious?" asked Jimmy.

"Never been more serious," said Mr. Nicholson. "I think we'll get on splendidly. Won't we, boy? It's been a while since I had a dog. So it's about time."

The cocker spaniel barked, his large brown eyes laughing.

Happiness filled Jimmy. He wouldn't have been surprised if he just floated away up over the treetops like a helium balloon cut free.

12

Shopping for Pets

At the strip mall, they pulled into the center of the parking lot, the stores in a half square around them. In the middle was a ten-foot Christmas tree decorated and lit.

"All right," called Blake. "Here are the presents for the tree!" He jumped out with the huge, floppy puppy. The rest of the kids tumbled out with their canines. The cats stared from cages, fearful, but curious. A couple cats batted through the wire at one another's bows.

After giving their shelter dogs to others to hold, Katie and Jimmy carefully unfolded a computer-generated sign Katie had run off at her family's hardware store yesterday. She'd colored it with markers.

"Looks great, Kate," said Melissa. She held a retriever mix--a dog the color of honey--and Katie's wire-haired wiener dog.

The sign read:

The Christmas Gift That Loves Back

Adopt a Dog or Cat

From the Farley Animal Hospital and Shelter

Katie had colored in the letters with red and green, like candy canes, and had drawn cats batting at the letters and dogs jumping from word to word.

"This is perfect," said Jimmy as they taped the banner on the outside of the horse trailer.

Katie beamed with pleasure and Jimmy decided she was prettier than knockout Anne at the animal hospital.

Mr. Nicholson and his black cocker spaniel, Noel—"What else can I call a Christmas dog?" he had asked—tended to Bess, pulling her out of the horse trailer and tying her up to the back of the trailer. He tossed a blanket over her harness to keep her warm in the brisk December air. Mr. Nicholson unsnapped Bess's bit and pulled it out of her mouth, then attached a nose bag with sweet feed inside for her to munch.

"Just like in old movies," said Lindsey, patting the muscled shoulder of Bess.

At first people coming or going to their cars pointed at the truck and trailer, exclaiming, "Look!" A couple adults called out, "Are you giving rides?"

Bess looked so festive, it was easy to think that people would assume that might happen.

"I'm afraid not," called Mr. Nicholson. "Something about business licenses."

"Is that true?" asked Jimmy, thinking rides would have been a good idea.

Mr. Nicholson nodded. "We don't have permission to give rides, only to be here to release pets for adoption." Dr. Smith had called yesterday to request permission. "Also I don't have insurance in case an accident happens."

"It gets complicated fast," said Jimmy.

"That it does," agreed Mr. Nicholson. "That it does."

A couple kids ran over to pet the horse. "Doggies!" yelled one kid. *That is for sure,* thought Jimmy. All kinds of dogs. Big ones, small ones, white ones, spotted ones.

"Heaps of dogs," said one kid, his front teeth missing.

"You want one?" asked Jimmy.

The kid's face lit up. "Yeah."

"Go ask your mom," said Jimmy.

Miracle of miracles, the kid came right back with his mother and they took a medium-sized black and tan female with a feathery tail that curled over her back.

Blake handed out a dog adoption certificate and the coupons and explained the dog was already spayed and given her shots.

"What a deal!" exclaimed the kid's mother.

When they left, Jimmy and Blake whooped for joy. "Our first," crowed Jimmy. "Hip hip hooray."

"Second one," reminded Mr. Nicholson patting Noel.

"Third one," said Katie. "Mom said I could give Bandy to my Great-Aunt Elizabeth."

Jimmy threw his arms around Lassie, pulled her up onto

81

her hind feet, and waltzed around in a circle with his dog.

Even though the sky darkened and the wind picked up, shoppers still gallantly trooped over to see the animals. Brave kids stroked Bess's big nose, then petted the dogs and looked at the cats.

Two older women took the beautiful Siamese. "A Christmas present to ourselves!" they exclaimed and carried the purring cat away.

By three o'clock two more cats had been adopted, an orange tiger-striped cat with six perfect toes on each paw, and a slender blue-gray. "He's probably part bloodhound," said Blake to the family who adopted a big floppy puppy. The little terrier Lindsey had held went to another family with two children.

"Don't worry, Honey," Melissa said to her retriever. "I bet you'll be adopted tomorrow." She turned to Jimmy. "I'll come until she's chosen."

"Me, too," said Alexander. His dog was a chow mix, complete with black tongue.

"Me, three," said Katie, patting the wiener dog.

"Tomorrow at the animal shelter, one o'clock?" asked Jimmy to Mr. Nicholson who said that was fine. Jimmy figured one more afternoon would do it for the rest of the animals. They'd all have homes for Christmas!

Jimmy's friends headed home. Blake and Jimmy rode in the back of the pickup with the remaining dogs and cats.

Mr. Nicholson drove them back to the animal hospital. As they wheeled into the parking lot of the hospital, Lassie stuck her nose out the back of the truck and barked.

"What, girl?" Jimmy untangled himself from dog legs and leashes and helped Katie and Blake unload the animals. Lassie, who was still barking, made him look up again.

A woman stood at the back door of the shelter. Next to her was a dog tied to the doorknob, and next to the dog was a guinea pig in a wire cage.

13

More Pets than Ever

Tuesday morning, Mr. Krebs was shoveling the snow from his driveway.

Jimmy knew what was coming, but he had to face it sometime. He picked up the morning newspaper, flinching when the bullet-words shot from the Krebs' yard to his.

"Did I see another dog at your house last night?" Mr. Krebs demanded, striding over to the low split-rail fence that separated their yards. Jimmy wished the rail was a thousand-foot-wide moat with alligators.

"Yes, but see, Mr. Nicholson and his dog are only staying with us until after Christmas," Jimmy explained. He felt like adding, "You remember, don't you, Mr. Grinch, that it's almost Christmas? Brotherly love and all that stuff?"

"That dog was barking all night long," complained Mr. Krebs. "I was awake for hours."

"It couldn't have been Noel," protested Jimmy. "He slept in the guest bedroom with Mr. Nicholson. We would have heard him bark." Jimmy remembered how Noel and

Lassie had played like puppies in the family room, chasing a ball around and around as if they were soccer stars. But no way could Mr. Krebs have heard them. Besides, they'd all gone to bed before eleven. So it couldn't have been the same dog.

"Well, someone's barking dog kept me awake," he said.

Like Jimmy was responsible for all the dogs in Farley. *So take a sleeping pill*, thought Jimmy. But he said, "I'm sorry about that, Mr. Krebs. But it wasn't Lassie or Noel."

Mr. Krebs grunted and moved off to finish shoveling snow. Jimmy hightailed it back to the house. He definitely felt sorry for little Megan, having to live with her grandfather.

As he closed the door behind him, he felt a twinge of guilt. He was developing a real attitude about Mr. Krebs. Dad had said something in his sermon last Sunday that had been working on him the past couple of days. He had said God isn't as interested in taking us out of difficult situations, as He is in developing character in us—Christlike character—through our difficult situations. Living next to an animal hater, Jimmy figured, was definitely a difficult situation. He wasn't sure how God would handle things if He were in Jimmy's shoes, but one thing Jimmy knew for sure, he had to work on his attitude.

That afternoon everybody met at the bouquet shopping area. There would be a different crowd here. The stores were a little more fancy.

The new dog, a male, had been given his vaccination last night, then bathed by Blake in the morning. The guinea pig was brushed, his cage tidied, then the girls tied a green ribbon around his neck, which he promptly chewed up.

"He probably thinks it was parsley or something because of the green color," said Jimmy.

Blake rolled his eyes. "Reality check, Jimmy. Animals are color-blind."

"Well, I don't think so."

"You're disagreeing with scientists?" asked Blake.

In other words, his father, thought Jimmy. But he repeated stubbornly, "I've seen Lassie react to color. She's not color blind."

"Then she's the only dog in the world who can see color," said Blake.

"Guys," said Katie. "Who cares? We've got work to do."

Lots of shoppers stopped by the new location near the Candy Works Factory and petted the animals. Someone wanted to take Bess.

"She's not up for adoption today, anyway," said Mr. Nicholson. "Ask me another day after she's been stubborn."

Jimmy buckled a small harness on a white Persian cat. He thought if he could let people pet the cats more easily, they might be more likely to take one home. The Persian seemed laid back enough to deal with strangers.

Jimmy walked with the Persian draped around his shoulders, strolling through the crowds outside shops on one side of the mall. Other kids walked dogs near the other shops.

Whenever someone showed interest in the cat, he went into his adoption pitch. However, today no one seemed to want an animal. *Maybe we should have stayed at the strip mall,* he thought. People were more interested there for some reason.

Jimmy waited to cross the parking lot back to the pickup to give the cat a break, when a cop cruiser inched by in the parking lot. In the backseat was a K-9 German Shepherd who burst into wild barks. Even with the windows up, Jimmy could tell the barks were loud and fierce.

The Persian, as if he'd suddenly woke from a spell and discovered himself outside perched on a strange boy's shoulders with a snapping dog after him, yowled and leaped straight up and off Jimmy's shoulders.

"Hey!" Jimmy shouted, startled. The cat was so quick that the leash slipped out of his hands. In one bound the cat had shot onto the nearest high object: the hood of the cop car.

The K-9 cop burst into a fresh frenzy of barking. As the cat hit the slick hood of the cruiser, he skidded like a beginning downhill skier on the advanced slopes. The cat yowled again, did a complete spin out, and slid off and over the hood of the cop car.

Inside the cruiser, the cop was laughing so hard that he

hit the horn. The cat shot straight up again, as high as the car window. The K-9 smashed into that side of the car, barking in most undignified tones, hoping that the officer would stop and let him tear this feline apart.

As the cat landed, Jimmy managed to scoop up the flailing animal, clutch him to his chest, and run for the truck. The cat had scratched his neck and hands. It was a good thing that he had his heavy winter coat on or Jimmy would have been mincemeat by now. So much for trying to get the public closer to the pets. It was dangerous!

Later in the afternoon, one family adopted the calico manx. She was the only animals adopted on Tuesday.

"I can't believe this," said Jimmy. "What happened?"

"Patience, boy, patience," said Mr. Nicholson. "In good time."

They couldn't take the animals out tomorrow because of the dress rehearsal, which Jimmy knew would drag on all afternoon. Then Thursday was his birthday. Great. He'd be working all day on his birthday, and no one even remembered.

Discouraged, Jimmy, Katie, and Blake packed up the animals and climbed into the back of Mr. Nicholson's truck. He drove them back to the rear of the shelter. When they arrived, Mr. Nicholson stopped and got out to open the gate that kept the public away from using this entrance. As he did this, a station wagon pulled up and honked. Jimmy half opened the back door of the truck and peered out. A kid rolled down the window and shouted, "Can you take our dogs? We're moving out of state and can't take them. We don't want them put to sleep."

"Sucker," hissed Blake as Jimmy jumped out of the truck to take the newcomers. Jimmy couldn't turn them down.

So they ended up with two more dogs than they had started with, even though they were a purebred pair of brindled boxers with homely but cute squashed faces.

Katie, Blake, and Jimmy unloaded the animals, fed them, and then settled them back in their kennels and tidied the cat cages.

"Hey, Mr. Nicholson," Blake yelled as the three climbed in the back of the truck to go home. "Could we drive around to the front of the shelter? I promised my dad that I would check the locks before going home tonight."

Mr. Nicholson nodded.

As they drove around to the front of the animal shelter, Jimmy took one look at the front door and groaned, "Oh no, not again!"

Backfiring Plans

"**C**an you believe it?" asked Katie after they'd fed and bedded down the newcomers.

"Yes, I believe it," said Jimmy. "But I don't like it."

Two dogs, a lop-eared rabbit, and, of all the crazy animals, a miniature Vietnamese pot-bellied pig had been tied outside to the front door, waiting in the cold. The pig had on an old sweatshirt that read: Go Hogs!

"I don't know how people can just leave animals out in the cold," Katie said to no one in particular. "It's cruel."

"This is getting real old," said Blake. "We're supposed to be getting rid of animals, not collecting them."

"Don't tell me," said Jimmy. "Inform the general public." Jimmy counted. "Our grand total is four cats, seven dogs, one rabbit, one guinea pig, and one small, fat pig."

"Don't talk about Katie like that," said Blake jokingly.

"I'm not fat!" she exclaimed.

"It's more in the piglike nose," agreed Jimmy as he held up his hands as if he were a photographer sizing up a shot.

Katie flew at him, pounding his arm with her fist. He held her off, laughing.

She backed up, hands on her hips. "I have an idea," she said suddenly. "Let's give them away. You know, late at night. Tie them to people's doors."

"Yeah, Mr. Krebs needs about three dogs and that pig," said Blake.

The rabbit was in a cardboard box so they put her in a cat cage with some hay. The pig was led snorting and snuffling into the one empty dog run. The dogs were put into runs, doubling them up when necessary. Jimmy didn't even want to say it out loud, but if they received any more animals they'd have to turn them away. There was no more room in the inn, so to speak.

He and Lassie walked home. Mr. Nicholson had driven the pickup to the church to work some more on toys.

The sky was gunmetal gray and overrun with clouds. Jimmy wished it would just blizzard and get it over with.

"This animal adoption thing is backfiring," Jimmy told Lassie as they turned down their street. She pressed her nose against his gloved hand and whined.

Jimmy opened his front door. Noel, flanked by a handsome beagle, greeted them. Mom and Sarah told him that two kids had come by their house earlier that day with the beagle, begging them to ask Jimmy to "please, please, please give our dog to a nice home." They couldn't keep him because their new stepmother was allergic to animals.

That's all I need, Jimmy thought, as he let the three dogs out into the backyard, praying Mr. Krebs wouldn't see the extra dog.

Lassie walked to the edge of the driveway. She stood with her slim head up, listening to something.

Noel and the beagle snuffled happily together, rooting through the layer of snow over the dead lawn. Jimmy crossed his arms over his chest and wondered again how in the world he was going to get rid of all the animals before Christmas. Mom had claimed him for all of Wednesday.

"I need your help for the pageant. I told you that last week," she had added a little crossly at breakfast.

He knew better than to argue with her when she was in that mood. Thursday was his birthday but he'd all but given up hope that anyone in his family even remembered. Friday was Christmas Eve. The pageant was seven in the evening. Maybe he could do a few hours of animal adoption in the morning, but he had a feeling Mom would nix that plan.

If only he could think of an idea that would make people want to take home pets for Christmas. Everything he thought of—classified ads in the newspaper, more flyers, different locations, a real parade—took time, something he didn't have.

Lassie whined, alerting. Jimmy crossed the lawn, tripping over the fawning beagle and the laughing Noel. "What, girl?" he asked her.

She stared across the street, and down a few houses. But he couldn't see anything different. He heard nothing unusual. A van drove past. Then a pickup truck backed out from the Andersons' directly across the street from the Harmons'. Across the street and next to the Andersons' was the Baxters' house, which had smoke curling from the chimney. The third house down was the Kincaids' who'd left their Christmas lights on all night. Jimmy especially liked the tiny white lights strung through the bushes and trees on their lawn.

But Lassie seemed to be looking beyond that to the old Campbells' place. It had been empty for months.

In the distance a dog barked, then broke into a mournful howl.

"That's it," said Jimmy. "I don't even want to think about another dog. Inside," he commanded his three charges. For once Lassie didn't quickly obey. She continued to stare down the street.

"Lassie, now," said Jimmy, a little sterner than before. "I refuse to think about taking any more strays. So get that idea out of your head." He finally grabbed her collar and hauled her back to the house.

Jimmy wiped all fourteen feet, including his own,

before they went inside. As he shut the front door, the wavering howl rippled through the streets.

Enough about stray dogs. He firmly turned his thoughts to his regular chores. He had made a promise to his dad before starting the adoption program that he would keep up with his chores, and he was falling behind on his promise. He needed to concentrate on getting as much done as possible today.

15

A Lousy Birthday

The rehearsal was perfectly awful. During the singing of "Silent Night," several angels tripped over their long robes and dominoed into each other in a massive angel pileup. One angel rolled off the stage, smashing his wings, yelling ferocious unangel words.

"Everyone take your places," said Mom for about the ninety-seventh time after she'd dusted off fallen angels and straightened their coat hanger-wings.

"Gonna put someone's eye out," muttered Blake. Jimmy grinned at his friend across the stage, Blake's royal crown's fake jewels glinting in the light. Blake was such a mother hen.

"I still think you ought to be Joseph," Jimmy called.

"Yeah, right. A black Joseph," said Blake. Kids around them giggled.

"No really, I have this theory," said Jimmy. "Later Joseph takes his family and flees to Egypt, right? So maybe he's got relatives there. So he could have been black."

"I just don't think Jesus had a black daddy," said Blake.

"Are you going to tell us next that Joseph helped build the pyramids?" Katie teased.

"It could have happened," said Jimmy, ducking as Katie grabbed the baby doll and tried to hit him over the head with it.

"Child abuse," yelled Jimmy.

Kids around them laughed. Mom roared at them to all "Be quiet!" She glared daggers at Jimmy.

It was dark by the time rehearsal was over.

Mom had retreated to Dad's office to sit in the soothing quiet, while Katie and Blake helped Jimmy ready the stage for Friday's performance. All the pageant kids had been picked up. When they were finally done, the three friends sat together in the pews.

"Now what?" asked Katie.

"We ought to flee to Egypt," said Jimmy.

"We ought to send all the shelter animals to Egypt," said Blake.

"Now there's an idea," said Jimmy.

"We'll send them first class," said Blake. "Excuse me, flight steward? This dog wanted a drink of water but there wasn't any in the toilet."

"Gross!" hollered Katie.

Jimmy couldn't stop thinking what to do next with the shelter animals. "I guess we should take the animals to the

Old West Shoppe tomorrow," said Jimmy. "People there are probably into animals cause the feed store and stuff is there."

Katie and Blake exchanged a glance. Jimmy caught it but didn't understand what was behind it, and he was too tired to ask what it was about. He figured they were sick of the pets. He knew he was. And that shocked him. Here he was the champion of animals, but he was wanting to give up so easily. He sighed. And worst of all, tomorrow was his birthday and no one even remembered.

Sure enough, the next morning when Jimmy went downstairs for breakfast no one said a word about his birthday. At first he was hurt, then angry. What was wrong with them? How many times did their only son, their eldest child, turn thirteen years old? He'd write a letter to the editor, complaining about parents who don't care. He'd sign the letter, "Neglected."

"Are you going to be gone all day, dear?" asked Mrs. Harmon.

Jimmy didn't even look at her. "Unless we adopt all the animals early," he said, shoving cold cereal into his mouth. Not even pancakes for breakfast. On special occasions Mom fixed fancy pancakes, such as blueberry or whipped cream and strawberries. All he got was colored cold cereal.

As fast as possible he got out of the house with Lassie at his heels. He went out the back door to avoid Mr. Krebs, who was shoveling snow again, probably just waiting to complain about the barking dog, which Jimmy did hear last night. Lassie's ears had pricked up every time she'd heard the dog as she lay beside Jimmy on the bed. He wished he knew what dogs said when they barked, for surely they did speak to one another. Sometimes he was pretty sure what Lassie said, but if he was honest, he was really only guessing.

Mr. Nicholson had already gone to church to finish mending the last of the toys. All the toys and food were being given to the firefighters to distribute on Friday—Christmas Eve. Mr. Nicholson said he would meet the kids about ten at the animal shelter.

Jimmy and Lassie jogged to the shelter and got there a few minutes before nine. Blake was already inside with Katie and they were blow-drying a dog Jimmy hadn't seen before.

"Another one tied to the door?" Jimmy asked wearily.

Katie nodded. "Just one this morning," she said, brightly.

Jimmy walked up to the dog. She looked like a German short-haired pointer. He petted her and she licked his hand. He wondered again how people could just get rid of their pets, like they were used furniture. His resolve strengthened again, he decided to help these animals find good homes, even on his birthday.

16

Trapped in a Zoo!

All day Jimmy and his friends, both human and animal, stood outside the Old West Shoppe, with its tack and feed store. Not one person took home an animal.

"I just can't believe it," Jimmy kept saying. Was God frowning on them? If God was, then what had he or any of them done wrong?

"Nothing," Mr. Nicholson kept saying. "You and your friends have done nothing wrong. This isn't about right or wrong. This is about being patient and waiting on the Lord."

"But Christmas Eve is tomorrow," said Jimmy. "The animals are supposed to be at their new homes."

Mr. Nicholson merely smiled and said quietly, "We can't force God's timing."

Well, personally, he thought God's timing stunk. What was he supposed to do with all these dogs and cats and other creatures?

Dr. Smith had told them this morning that if they didn't adopt out some of the animals today, the kids would have to take several dogs home. The shelter had become too crowded. Not safe. Not sanitary. And not fair to the cramped dogs.

With a heavy sigh, Jimmy figured he could take three dogs and let them stay in the basement. Their house was already full with Lassie and Noel. He had a feeling Mom wouldn't appreciate more dogs in the house. Their basement was partially finished so it wasn't like the dogs were in an icy cold dungeon. He prayed Mr. Krebs wouldn't see him with three more dogs. Because if Mr. Krebs did, he would probably call the pound to take Jimmy away.

At this point Jimmy almost wanted to be taken away.

About three o'clock snow started falling. Not just a gentle sprinkle, but a good dumping that meant nasty weather was happening.

"Let's go," said Jimmy after a half hour of standing out in the blowing, wet stuff. Some of the short-haired dogs were shivering. He hadn't thought to bring old shirts and sweaters for them. So much to remember.

As they were loading up, a family—a dad, a mom, a boy about ten and a girl seven, came over and admired the pair of boxers.

The father said, "I had a boxer as a boy. Great dogs. We'd be interested in adopting one of the boxers."

"Just one?" asked Jimmy. "They've been together since puppies." That's what their original family had said. "I think they would miss each other."

The father got impatient. "Well, all we can take is one. Can we take it or not?"

Jimmy sadly shook his head. "I'm sorry. We can't separate them."

The father stormed off, the family in his wake. Jimmy wondered if he was as stupid as he felt.

They loaded the animals in silence. Blake rode up front with Mr. Nicholson. Jimmy and Katie sat in the back with dogs everywhere, mostly vying to sit in their laps.

Jimmy put his arms around the two ugly, but cute Boxers. He'd take them home, along with the new German short-haired pointer. Katie and Honey, the retriever, had been a couple since the first day. Poor Rags was jealous.

"You did the right thing, Jim," said Katie seriously. "Not to separate those two."

"I hope so," said Jimmy. "I read this story in the newspaper about twin girls who were up for adoption, and they actually gave them to different families. That doesn't seem right, does it?"

"It doesn't," said Katie. "But I guess if it's a matter of no one adopting them, it's better for them."

"There has to be a family out there to adopt these two," insisted Jimmy. "All of these are great dogs. We just have to find the right families." *But time is up,* he thought. *Tomorrow is Christmas Eve. There's no time left to try.* He mentally kicked himself for not running a classified ad about the animals. He just hadn't taken the time to do it. Now he understood when adults complained about not having enough time.

For a while, he dozed. The warm dog bodies comforted him and the soothing motion of the truck lulled him to sleep.

A blast of cold air in his face startled him full awake. Katie had opened the back door and was peering out the back, letting the winter blast into the pickup.

"Aren't we at the animal hospital yet?" Jimmy asked.

She pulled her head back in. Snowflakes clung to her russet hair and her eyelashes. "It's snowing pretty good. For some reason we're over on Maple Ave." That wasn't near the hospital. Jimmy untangled himself from the boxers and climbed over dogs and cat cages to the front. He knocked on the glass window and Blake slid the window open.

Blake was bundled so only his eyes showed over his red scarf. He had dressed for the weather.

"What's happening?" asked Jimmy.

"Traffic accident," Blake said. "We're being detoured."

Oh, great. Here they were trapped in a pickup, in a blizzard, with ten dogs, four cats, a rabbit, a guinea pig, and one pot-bellied pig. What a zoo!

"Is it my imagination," he asked Katie, "or does it smell in here?"

She giggled. "I wish it was only your imagination."

Jimmy knocked on the window again. Blake slid it open.

"I think our friends here are going to need a potty break soon," Jimmy said.

Blake talked to Mr. Nicholson, then turned back to Jimmy. "We're closest to your house right now," said Blake. "I think we're going to stop there until the traffic unsnarls and the snow quits."

Jimmy sat back, unable to help laughing. Now they'd be stuck at his house in a blizzard with ten dogs, four cats, a rabbit, a guinea pig, and a pot-bellied pig!

17

A Time of Miracles

They finally turned into the Harmons' backyard. Someone, Dad maybe, had left the gate open for them. Bess had been plunging through the deepening snow so she was sweating. Some sweat would turn to ice crystals, then melt during more exertion and thicken to ice crusts along her back. Mini-icicles hung from the harness.

Jimmy jumped out and headed for the house as Blake and Katie supervised dogs relieving themselves in the yard.

The house was dark, which surprised Jimmy. It had to be after five. Usually Mom had dinner going and ready by five-thirty or six. Pastor Harmon worked at the church until six. Maybe the snow had held them up too.

He hadn't brought his house keys, so he squeezed through the narrow basement window. He switched on the lights and opened the door to the finished part of the basement. It had a wall heater so he turned it on. He took down a bin of old towels to dry off wet animals and laid down newspapers on the cement floor for the "bathroom" area, hoping the dogs were housebroken, but who knew?

Then he opened the outside basement door and began carrying in cages of cats. He wished he could let them out, but even though the dogs had quit barking at them in the cages, he figured night-long chases would ensue or worse a feeding frenzy. Dogs tended to get carried away when in packs.

Please don't let Mr. Krebs see us, Jimmy prayed as he toted cages. If his neighbor saw them with all these animals. . . .

He didn't even want to think about that. For once he was thankful the snowfall was as heavy as a curtain. He could hardly see his own house from the corral.

Mr. Nicholson was rubbing down Bess. Katie, Blake, and Jimmy led the dogs into the basement and set about finding bowls and pans to water and feed the dogs.

Mom's summer gardening pots had pie tins as bases, so Jimmy washed them in the laundry sink and filled up several with water. In the downstairs pantry they had bulk items of food, including several fifty pound bags of dog food for Lassie, meant to last all winter.

Oh, well, thought Jimmy. I can't let these guys starve. So he tore open the first bag and laid out nearly twenty pounds of kibble in pie tins.

Now for the cats. He poked around in the pantry and found some cans of tuna, opened them, and soon the cats were purring and scarfing up. The rabbit and guinea pig ate handfuls of Bess's hay. Now for the pig. What did pigs eat?

Dog food as it turned out. The pig waddled around from pan to pan, snuffling, pushing his weight against the nearest dog, gobbling a mouthful, then moving on to another pie tin.

"Kind of pigging out, isn't he?" asked Katie.

Jimmy set down another pan heaped with kibble.

Finally they got all the animals, including Bess, settled in, warm, dry, and eating contentedly.

"I used to want to live on a farm," said Jimmy. "But I think I'm having second thoughts."

"Come live at my dad's animal hospital, " offered Blake. "That will really cure you."

"I feel like we *have* been living there," said Jimmy.

With Mr. Nicholson, Lassie, and Noel behind them, the kids trooped upstairs. Jimmy opened the basement door into the still, dark house.

"This is weird," he muttered. "Where is everyone?" The luminous clock in the kitchen read ten after six. He started into the dark family room, with Katie, Blake, and Lassie crowding behind him. Suddenly the lights flared on.

His parents, Sarah, and about thirty kids shouted, "Surprise! Happy Birthday!"

About an hour into the birthday party someone, probably Blake, let all the shelter dogs upstairs. Soon Jimmy's party was overrun with barking dogs, yelling kids, and so much laughter and happiness Jimmy could hardly believe it.

"I thought you forgot," he kept saying to his mom and dad.

Sarah clapped her hands. "Good! We wanted to worry you!"

"Thanks, Sarah." He punched her arm.

She socked him back. "Happy Birthday, big brother."

Mrs. Harmon had fixed his favorite dinner for everyone, lasagna dripping with cheese; soft, warm garlic bread oozing with butter; and best of all, a chocolate cake with swirls of thick frosting.

Mom put her arms around him and said with tears, "I can't believe my baby is a teenager."

"Aw, Mom," he wriggled out of her arms, his face bright red. But he gave her a quick kiss.

After dinner and cake, with Lassie sitting beside him, Jimmy opened presents. His parents had remembered the shoes. Perfect running shoes. Blake had given him some computer software games, plus one disk that was designed to help him run a kennel more efficiently.

"Oh, no," Mrs. Harmon said as a couple of chasing dogs nearly knocked her down. "Those dogs are going back as soon as the snow quits."

Katie had given him a cable-knit sweater, sort of like what he'd finally chosen for her Christmas present, so he didn't feel so weird about giving it to her. "I helped Gran knit it," she confessed.

"Really?" he held it up. It was royal blue and scarlet, their school colors. "You did a great job, Katie." She beamed at him and he beamed right back.

Other kids from the youth group and school had brought presents too. He'd never gotten so many presents in his life. And he'd thought no one remembered! Mr. Nicholson handed him a box with a simple ribbon wrapped around it. "Something I made," he said with a smile.

Eagerly Jimmy cut the ribbon. Inside he found a collie, painted perfectly like Lassie. "You made this?" he asked, amazed. It was like a work of art, or something.

Everyone crowded around. The dog was lifelike. Even Lassie sniffed it curiously as if she thought it would jump up and bark at her.

"Carved it out of white cedar," Mr. Nicholson said.

"That is something," said Pastor Harmon, admiringly.

"You should see some of the toys Mr. Nicholson has mended," said Mrs. Harmon. "They are practically miraculous."

Jimmy smiled to himself. It was that time of year, wasn't it? The time of miracles.

18

Two Lost Girls

Over a foot of snow had fallen during the night. In some places the snow had drifted to nearly four feet high.

"How are we going to get the animals back?" wondered Jimmy. The snowplows were busy, but the smaller streets were the last to be plowed.

Jimmy quickly donned his jacket and hat and went out to join his dad and Mr. Nicholson who were shoveling.

From an upstairs window at the Krebs, Jimmy saw Megan, watching. He waved and she waved back. But she didn't come outside. Probably forbidden to talk to him.

When they finished shoveling, Mr. Nicholson and Jimmy loaded up all the animals, except the boxer pair and the German shorthair. He left Lassie, hoping she would be a calming influence on the new dogs left behind.

They drove off, Megan still watching. Jimmy waved again, but the little girl just sat there motionless.

Instead of going back home after the hospital, Mr. Nicholson drove Jimmy to the church. The pageant wasn't scheduled to start until six. But there was still some last-minute decorating to do. Mrs. Harmon and Sarah were already there when they entered the church.

About two, Mr. Nicholson offered to take Jimmy home to get his costume.

"How does Bess keep from slipping on slippery roads?" asked Jimmy as they drove along the streets.

"I'll show you at home," Mr. Nicholson said.

When they arrived, Mr. Nicholson and Jimmy walked out to the shed to check on Bess. Mr. Nicholson picked up Bess's front hoof and showed Jimmy the cleats in her shoes. "Also, I spray nonstick cooking spray in her hooves."

"So the snow doesn't ball up in her feet?"

"Exactly."

Jimmy thought Mrs. Nicholson must be one of the smartest men on earth. He knew such practical things.

As they started up the back stairs of the house, an all-too-familiar voice called Jimmy's name.

Reluctantly he turned. Mr. Krebs was staring at the Harmons' back gate as if he were already thinking about something else.

Jimmy started to say, "The dogs were just here for the night because of the snow," when he realized Mr. Krebs was saying something about Megan—about Megan being gone.

"Gone?" Jimmy repeated. "I saw her in the window this morning."

"She's gone now," said Mr. Krebs. "Her grandmother put her down for a nap about one-thirty and when she went to wake her up, Megan was gone."

A chill clutched Jimmy. How could she be gone?

Mr. Nicholson asked, "Have you called the sheriff?"

Mr. Krebs nodded grimly. "I did. They've already begun looking. When I saw you folks drive up, I thought I'd ask if you've seen her." Then he said in a lower voice, "She's been talking for days about your dogs. I thought maybe she'd come over here to see them."

A pang struck Jimmy. "I'll check the house." Maybe somehow she'd climbed in through the basement window. Maybe she had spied Jimmy trying to get in that way last night.

"Keep your eyes peeled," added Mr. Krebs.

"We will," said Jimmy.

"We'll pray she returns safely," Mr. Nicholson said.

Jimmy thought Mr. Krebs would growl something about not to bother with the prayer stuff, but instead the grouchy old man just said, "Thank you kindly."

Maybe the old geezer has a heart after all, thought Jimmy amazed.

Jimmy checked the basement but the Boxers and the short-haired pointer were alone. They barked madly around him. He couldn't tell if Megan had been here or not.

Funny, Lassie wasn't here. Maybe Mom had let her upstairs

115

after all. So he went upstairs. Mr. Nicholson was inside the house already with Noel jumping on his legs. Still no Lassie.

"Did you let Lassie outside?" asked Jimmy.

A puzzled look came into Mr. Nicholson's eyes. "She didn't come to the door with Noel."

"She's not in the basement, either," said Jimmy.

Mr. Nicholson looked as alarmed as Jimmy felt. Instantly he just knew, Megan and Lassie were together. But where and why?

"Maybe we can see her tracks," Mr. Nicholson suggested. "The snow stopped falling a while ago."

They went back outside and saw some dog prints, more like holes than paw prints in the soft snow. They began at the back door. Apparently Mom had let her into the house and then out again into the backyard. Lassie had probably unlocked the yard gate herself. On the street, the wind was blowing and the snowplow had removed any tracks Lassie could have made in the street. They couldn't tell if she'd gone next door to the Krebs' or if Megan had come over to meet her.

"Now what?" asked Jimmy.

"Let's get ready for your pageant, and on our way we'll scout around a little."

19

The Song

They drove back to church the long way, winding up and down some of the streets near Jimmy's neighborhood. Jimmy called Lassie's name. Megan's, too. Nothing.

About halfway to the church, a sheriff's car stopped them, and the deputy began to tell them about Megan's being lost.

"I think she's with my dog," Jimmy blurted out. The deputy allowed him to explain all the ins and outs of Megan's and Lassie's relationship. He handed Jimmy his business card with his home phone number on it.

"Any more ideas come to you or if you see something, let me know. Any time day or night," said the man. He waved and drove off.

"We'd better hurry to church," said Mr. Nicholson. "It's getting late."

Jimmy bit his lip. "I don't want to be there. Someone else can play Joseph. We have to find Megan and Lassie."

Mr. Nicholson said gently, "I don't think anyone at this

late time can learn your song."

"They can skip the song," said Jimmy. "It's no big deal. Like Joseph really sang a song after Jesus was born. He was probably in shock and just wanted a good night's sleep."

Mr. Nicholson laughed. "That may be the truth, but a lot of people are depending on you to be there tonight."

Jimmy sighed. "I guess so." Mom would utterly kill him if he didn't show up. "Okay," he said, "but right after it's over, I'm coming back to look until I find her. .. . them."

"I'll be right there with you," said Mr. Nicholson, pushing the gas peddle to make the truck go faster.

Jimmy turned to the old man. "Thank you."

Ironically the pageant went the smoothest that he could remember. Everything fell into place perfectly: no angels piled up; no shepherd cried that he wanted his mother; Wanda played slowly, like the music was written.

When it was his turn to sing with Katie, his heart and throat seized up for a moment, not from fear or stage fright, but from pure sadness.

He and Mr. Nicholson had agreed not to say anything about Megan or Lassie until after the program. Then they'd invite people to help them look. They both felt in a weird way that that was what God wanted them to do.

Since the sheriff's people had dispatched a search team to begin looking, people from church would probably just get in their way. But later tonight if officials hadn't found Megan and Lassie, then they would need the help to span greater areas.

Jimmy and Katie first sang their lines together, then Katie sang her solo. Then his turn came.

He stepped forward, lights in his eyes, brilliant like the star of Bethlehem must have been. His throat relaxed, his mouth opened. The song tumbled out:

"A wanderer am I; my son will be too.

Hiding, but never completely in fear of man,

The Lord takes my infant son in His hand,

And will guide Him all His days through."

The last lingering notes of the song rained softly down over the packed congregation. For a moment no one in the audience stirred, then the clapping began and exploded. Jimmy and Katie grinned at each other.

As much as he liked knowing people enjoyed his singing, he just wanted to burst from the building to look for Lassie. Of course, he didn't. Instead he slowly turned and took his place beside the cradle—where he belonged.

The last of the pageant slipped away like water in a stream. Jimmy waited, a still figure as if fashioned out of stone.

Katie whispered, "Are you okay?" Maybe he looked sick or pale. How did she know? But friends were like that, aware when something different was going on.

He was afraid to answer, for if he opened his mouth again, he feared he'd start yelling Lassie's name and be unable to stop. He just gave a little shake of his head and tried to tell her with his eyes that he'd explain as soon as he could. She settled back on her heels, seeming to understand.

Finally the pageant with its sharp, sweet pine-bough scent and stuffy warmth of many bodies, and the golden songs of love, joy, and yes, pain, was over. He almost toppled as he relaxed the hold he'd had on his muscles to keep himself from running off.

The thought jumped into his head that a lot of pain had happened on the first Christmas. The pain of no room for the tired travelers. The pain of loneliness, for both the shepherds, and for Joseph and Mary. The pain of child-birth. The pain of knowing the difficult road ahead. For a brief moment he thought he sensed how Joseph must have really felt in trying to care for his young wife, his newborn son that wasn't even his own flesh and blood, yet was greater than any biological child could be.

Dad quietly told the congregation about Megan being gone. Apparently he had just called the sheriff's office, and they still hadn't found her.

"She's been missing since between two and three this afternoon," Pastor said. "And with the temperature dropping, we're concerned she may be outside. An hour ago it was nine degrees, with the windchill factor making it about ten below. The Krebs were pretty certain Megan had on her parka and boots when she left. Also there's the possibility that she was or had been with Lassie, who is also missing. If anyone wants to help, go directly to the incidence command post at the Krebs' house." Then Dad led them in a prayer and everyone filed out quietly.

Mr. Nicholson immediately drove Jimmy, Katie, and Blake straight over to the Krebs' house. Dad said he'd come over after wrapping things up at church and taking Mom and Sarah home.

With his friends, Jimmy jumped out of the wagon and they ran to the Krebs' house, which was completely lit up.

Mr. Krebs opened the door, his stern, wrinkled face old and defeated looking.

"We're here to help look," said Jimmy. "Some other people from church are behind us."

"Come inside," said Mr. Krebs gruffly. "We still haven't found her."

20

Whimper on the Wind

"**W**e've looked quickly in the neighborhoods near here," explained Captain Schultz, a tall, heavyset man with streaks of gray in his short, brown hair. He had a walrus mustache that twitched when he talked.

"What you can do is break into groups of three or four and search more carefully. You don't need to knock on neighbors' doors. We explained to the neighbors we'd be looking most of the night around their houses again if we didn't find her. Many children will hide when they are lost. Even if you call their name, they stay hidden and don't answer. So look in any sheds, wood piles, anywhere that a small child could possibly squeeze herself into," he said. "Any questions?"

Behind Jimmy, Pastor Harmon had walked into the house and asked, "Any possibility that she went with someone?"

Captain Schultz said grimly, "There's certainly that possibility. We have roadblocks up all over town."

Jimmy knew they meant that possibly someone snatched Megan—a gross and awful thought. But something inside him persisted in thinking she was with Lassie. And Lassie would never let any stranger take Megan. Not while Lassie lived at least.

Dad took Jimmy's arm, and to Jimmy's surprise Mr. Krebs volunteered to partner up with the two of them. Dad had gotten two flashlights from the house and handed one to Jimmy.

Mr. Nicholson put his hand on Jimmy's shoulder. His other hand had Noel on a leash. "We'll be looking, too, son."

They slipped out into the bitter cold night. The harsh wind seemed to rob any of the magic or miracle that had existed earlier in the night. Jimmy asked himself," "If God didn't answer my prayer about the animals, why do I think He'll answer my prayer about Megan?" He was afraid of the answer.

Snow crunched under their feet. Flurries of snow, caught momentarily in house lights, sparkled. A little voice inside Jimmy said flatly, "God has turned His back, hasn't He?"

Another part of him hastily said, "It just looks that way. God always comes through, even though it can be different than what you expect."

Jimmy sighed heavily, his breath streaming out white and thick as fog. He didn't want to debate with himself. He just wanted to find Megan and Lassie. *That would be the best Christmas present of all,* he thought. I wouldn't care if I didn't get any Christmas present, except finding them.

He found his heart ached equally for his collie and for the little girl.

Dad, Jimmy, and Mr. Krebs crossed the street and carefully began to walk into backyards and sideyards, looking in tool sheds, gardening sheds, in woodpiles, playhouses, dog houses. Jimmy even climbed up into a covered two-story treehouse, pretty elaborate, complete with little table and stools. But no Megan.

As he leaned out of the treehouse, the wind blasted him between the naked branches. On the wind came the whimper of a dog. Or was it a little kid? He held his breath, listening hard. Or was it even a whimper? Maybe just the wind moaning as it slid over icy rooftops.

Dad's flashlight beam skidded up the tree trunk and struck Jimmy in the face. He closed his eyes, like he had at church, and again wondered if the star of Bethlehem had blinded onlookers. "You're blinding me!"

Dad moved the beam. "Sorry."

"Did you see something?" asked Mr. Krebs.

"Thought I heard someone crying." He didn't say a dog's cry, knowing Mr. Krebs wouldn't appreciate his divided interest.

"Where?" Mr. Krebs practically started up the tree.

"I'm not sure. The wind's blowing the sound around." Jimmy waited another minute, hoping he'd hear the whimper again, but he didn't.

They started to check the next house. The porch light was on and no one seemed home. They let themselves in the side yard and walked throughout the backyard, their lights darting. Jimmy called Lassie's name and Megan's name, holding his breath listening.

Overhead clouds raced like a ragged herd of silent buffalo across snowy plains. The sliver of the moon gleamed out of a rip in the clouds. Jimmy wished he could funnel the moonlight into a spotlight.

This backyard was overgrown with hedges of evergreens. They poked through the snow-hatted bushes, but the branches were too dense even for a little girl to hide among.

Then as Jimmy held his face to the brittle, cold wind, again came the whimper. He hopped onto the wooden side fence and looked in the next backyard. Now he thought the cry came from the west.

The next house to check was the vacant house. The Campbells were an elderly couple who had moved to a retirement home about two months ago. The house was in poor shape, he'd heard, so it wasn't put up for sale yet. He wondered if Megan had gone inside. Maybe, to get out of the cold. Would Lassie have gone with her?

One way to find out.

"I think I heard the cry again," said Jimmy. "The Campbells' house is empty. Maybe we should look inside it."

Mr. Krebs's eyes brightened for a moment. "But why would she go to a vacant house?"

Probably to escape you, Jimmy thought out of habit, but he really didn't feel quite so antagonistic toward the older man. Mr. Krebs obviously cared for the little girl, even if he was harsh with her. He was just harsh with everyone.

As they quickly trampled to the vacant house, Dad prayed a quick prayer out loud. Jimmy didn't care if Mr. Krebs didn't like church, God, or prayer. They needed all the help they could get if they were going to find Megan alive.

Corner Snow Pile

Dad tried the front door, but not surprisingly, it was locked. They continued along the wraparound porch, peering in dirt-streaked, cobwebby windows. Mr. Krebs called Megan's name several times, his voice fading. Heavy snow piled up around the house and climbed up the porch sides. No answer. Not even the alleged whimpering Jimmy had thought he heard.

Jimmy checked windows in case the little girl had climbed inside one, but they were securely latched storm windows. There was no way she'd get in unless she broke one and that wasn't likely. She didn't seem the type.

The backyard was plain. Low bushes and a couple of bare trees scattered in the snow-filled yard. A low, stone fence off to one side framed what once was a herb or vegetable garden. Not a place for a child, even a small child, to hide. It was all too barren.

Dad tugged at a door of the storm shelter twenty feet from the house.

"She's terrified of cellars," said Mr. Krebs. "I don't think she'd go into one. I'll check around the other side of the house."

Dad gave Jimmy a look. Jimmy knew what he was thinking and it made his stomach turn. Bodies could be thrown down a cellar or a storm shelter. *Please God,* he thought. *Let her be safe.*

Dad scraped snow from the cellar door and hauled it open. They both shone their lights inside. The cellar was small and cramped. Canned food and plastic jugs of water were stored on two wooden shelves.

Jimmy climbed down and searched quickly behind the ladder, under the cot, and in a small wooden trunk filled with bedding. No body, thank God. Wearily he and Dad closed the door, latching it carefully. "Ought to lock it," said Dad. "For safety's sake. I'll come back tomorrow with a lock."

They started back around the house when a shout came from Mr. Krebs.

They ran.

Standing in the driveway, a street light's hazy yellow light shining over her, was Lassie. Mr. Krebs was bent over her, actually stroking her dirty fur.

"Lassie!" Jimmy ran to his dog and flung his arms around her. She whined and wriggled in his arms. "Oh, Lassie, where have you been?" he whispered.

To his amazement, Mr. Krebs was echoing his words in a hoarse voice, "Lassie, where is my little girl?"

"Where did she come from?" asked Pastor Harmon.

"She just appeared," said Mr. Krebs. "I was walking along the porch, trying the windows on the other side of the house, when I just saw her in front of the house."

Jimmy studied his dog. Her fur was snow dusted, but mostly her fur was dirty, as if she'd been rolling in dust. Where in the world did she find dust in this snowbound neighborhood?

All of a sudden it clicked. The dust. The whimpers. The strange dog barking at night.

Jimmy turned to Mr. Krebs excitedly. "Mr. Krebs, did you ever find the barking dog? The one keeping you awake at night?"

His heavy brows creased. "What difference does that make?"

"I think it might."

Instead of his usual continuing argument, he answered simply, "Yes, I did find it. This afternoon. It was barking and I called animal control. The dog had been in front of this house." His voice trailed off in puzzlement as if the answer were in front of him but he couldn't quite grasp it.

Jimmy frantically fit pieces of the puzzle together, trying to fashion the correct picture. "Did Megan see the animal - control people come for the dog?" he asked.

"I don't know," said Mr. Krebs. "She was down for her nap. At least she was supposed to be. We don't know exactly when she climbed out her window."

If the barking dog was taken by the animal control, why would Megan also be gone? Did she try to follow the animal-control truck? No, if Lassie was here, Megan must be somewhere nearby.

"Lassie, where's Megan?" Jimmy asked. "Go get her. Get Megan."

The collie whined, her brown eyes anxious. She trotted to the corner of the porch. Snow was piled up to the edge of the peeling, white porch top. The railing and slats were splintering and a few slats were missing. Lassie scratched at the snow pile against the porch corner. Jimmy moved near her when a saucer-sized plop of snow fell on Jimmy's head, knocking off his hat.

The roof was heavy with snow. Wind swirled more unstable snow piles to the ground. In fact, a large area of the roof was almost cleared as if someone had swept off a portion of it.

"That's it!" said Jimmy excitedly, and he began to dig at the drift. Lassie barked and joined in digging. Jimmy cried, "Megan's under the house!"

22

Midnight Music

Dad immediately dug his hands into the snow. Soon the porch corner was exposed. Mr. Krebs held the lights, his hands trembling so the beams jiggled. Along the chipped, white siding, a rectangular opening gaped. The metal screen was missing. Jimmy shone his light inside. In the dust beyond were many dog prints and child prints.

"Megan," called Jimmy softly. The area under the porch was long and their flashlights fell into darkness.

Lassie whined softly. Inside came a return whimpering.

"Megan," cried Mr. Krebs.

Still the child didn't answer with words, but the whimpering continued, a many-voiced whimper.

"That's not Megan, that noise came from puppies" exclaimed Jimmy. Lassie gave a bark and wriggled through the opening, her plume tail flicking in Jimmy's face.

"Puppies!" said Mr. Krebs, disappointed.

Jimmy and Dad exchanged glances. Dad said, "I bet Megan is with the puppies." Jimmy nodded. He thought so too. Mr. Krebs looked unbelieving, as if his granddaughter wouldn't associate with dogs.

"Can you fit through the opening, Jim?" asked Dad.

"I think so," said Jimmy. "But not with my jacket on." He pulled off his heavy parka and his thick sweater. The cold was penetrating. *I just have to hurry*, he told himself. He gripped his flashlight in his teeth and poked his head into the opening. Then one shoulder, then the other shoulder, scraping the top of his arm as he slid in. The rest of him slipped in more easily and he tumbled onto the soft dirt under the house.

Lassie brushed against him as if to say, "This way." Jimmy crouched, ducking his head. The clear space was about four feet high. He banged his head on a cracked, hanging beam.

"Ouch," he said as Lassie urged him deeper under the porch. Great, his luck the porch would collapse on him.

Then half way across the length of the house his light fell on Megan. She sat ram rod still, wide eyed, mouth in an O and puppies spilling across her lap.

"Megan," he whispered. "Are you okay?"

"Is she there?" called Pastor Harman.

"Megan, honey," said Mr. Krebs, his voice breaking.

Jimmy stared at the little girl as tears welled in her eyes. He told her softly, "I have to say yes. They are so worried."

She gave a tiny nod.

"She's here," Jimmy called over his shoulder. "She seems okay. She's got puppies with her. The dog's puppies that the animal-control people took this afternoon." He turned back to Megan, "Right?"

She nodded again. Two dark-furred puppies, the length of his forearm, slept in her lap, half under her jacket. She had brought a blanket with her and three other puppies, lighter in color, were wrapped under it. A half-empty jug of milk sat beside her, partially frozen.

"You thought pretty fast, didn't you?" asked Jimmy. "Getting all this stuff before you climbed out your window?"

Lassie laid down, curling up beside the puppies on the blanket, just like she belonged there, which, Jimmy admitted, she did. The puppies awoke, crawled out of the blanket, whimpering, and tangled themselves in her long fur. She licked them.

"I would have come back with them, but all these people were looking for me," Megan whispered. Her face was tear streaked and dirty. "If they found me with the puppies, I know Grandfather would just call the animal shelter, just like he did for the mama dog."

"This time I won't let him," said Jimmy fiercely. "I'll take care of the puppies. Lassie and I will." He thought, half amused, *What's five more puppies?*

Megan gave a big sigh, stirring the pups in her lap. She said, "I've got the shivers and my stomach is hungry.

I missed Christmas Eve, too, didn't I?"

Jimmy glanced at his watch. "Actually you have one hour and five minutes until midnight." He paused for a moment. "You know, if it wasn't for you these pups would have died. You've been kind of a guardian angel to them."

"Do you think so?" Her eyes were glistening. "I love them so much. When I found them, I couldn't leave them out in the cold."

"It's a good thing you were here," he said softly. "But now it's time to go home. Are you ready?".

She simply held out her arms. Carefully Jimmy rewrapped the puppies in the blanket beside Lassie. Awkwardly he picked up Megan, still having to bend over for the ceiling was low. She trustingly put her arms around his neck and clung tightly. Her warm body felt good against his jacketless body.

Jimmy helped her out through the opening. Dad and Mr. Krebs's hands reached for her. The harsh gasps of someone sobbing who wasn't used to crying came to him.

Jimmy went back for the blanket of puppies and cradled them against his chest. Lassie finally followed, her duty done, her human and canine children rescued.

Back at the Krebs', Megan lay in her grandfather's arms. The paramedics checked the child over and pronounced her fine. "A little dehydrated but not the worse for wear, considering her exposure to the cold."

"Lassie kept me warm," Megan explained several times. "Me and the puppies."

Mrs. Krebs took Megan upstairs to bathe her and put her to bed. As Dad and Jimmy were leaving, arms still full of puppies, Mr. Krebs stopped them, looking a little uneasy. "Thank you," he said, his eyes still wet. "I was wondering if I could ask another favor."

"Sure," said Dad.

"Could I, we, have one of the puppies? For Megan. To make up for the mother dog?"

Jimmy almost laughed to himself. Christmas Eve was a time for miracles! "Here, pick," he said opening the fold of blanket, showing the fat and sassy puppies. Their mother had taken good care of them even under poor circumstances.

Mr. Krebs didn't stroke the puppies, but stared at them, seeing something else. "You know I wasn't being completely heartless," he said. "The mother dog had been hit by a car. The animal control said she was severely injured."

"No wonder she was barking," said Jimmy. "She was asking for help." And no one helped her except a little girl.

Mr. Krebs finally touched one puppy with medium-length fur, the color of warm gingerbread. "Her color is a little like Lassie's, isn't it?"

"Megan will like that," said Jimmy, encouragingly.

"Yes." Mr. Krebs picked up the puppy in his big, veined

hands like he might hold a squash. The pup whimpered. Then Mr. Krebs held it against his chest. "Thank you," he said. "I think I have a few things to learn about puppies." He turned and hurried upstairs.

Jimmy looked at his dad and smiled.

"Come on, son," said Dad. "It's late."

They crunched home through the snow. After bedding down the puppies in a cardboard box in his room, Jimmy brushed Lassie's tangled and dirty fur.

It was almost midnight. He wondered if Megan was fast asleep or snuggling with her new puppy. He decided the latter was more likely. She'd be awake.

Quietly he pulled on his parka and slipped silently outside with Lassie.

The sky had cleared some, clouds bunching on the eastern horizon, as if the wind were herding them away. A few brave stars peeked out and the curve of the first quarter moon cut through thinning clouds.

Jimmy and Lassie stopped under Megan's window. He rolled a soft snowball and threw it up at her window. Thump. He bent over to make another when a face appeared. Megan pushed open the glass. "I got a new puppy," she called down.

"I know," he said. "Now, you'll have your very own dog to look after."

She held up her puppy in triumphantly. He gave her a

thumbs-up sign, waved, and started back. He'd leave her alone with her new puppy.

Somehow he felt that tonight all was well with the world. Isn't it amazing how a few days can change everything when God is in control. To think that God provided a puppy for Megan and a change of heart for Mr. Krebs. He had helped them find Megan before she'd frozen to death, and had kept Lassie safe. All miracles!

Jimmy stood on the fence top and waved. Megan waved back. He and Lassie went home, and it was as if he heard the soft sound of voices singing praises to the Lord.

23

Follow The Star

The next morning after opening the presents under the tree, Dad said, "Look at this." He held up the front page of the *Daily Farley Tribune*. A headline read: "Lost Girl Found: Kept Safe by Dog." Next to the headline was a photo of Megan in Mr. Krebs's arms. Dad read:

"Lost girl, Megan Krebs, 7, was found after reportedly being missing for six hours yesterday. She was found under a vacant house, caring for 5 motherless puppies, and was herself being warmed and cared for by Lassie, a collie owned by Jimmy Harmon, 13."

"They even got my age right," exclaimed Jimmy.

Sarah rolled her eyes. "Like that's important."

"It's important to me," insisted Jimmy.

Dad read on. The story explained how they'd finally found Megan. And how Megan was keeping one of the puppies, but Jimmy was taking the rest of the puppies. The story also told about Jimmy's adoption efforts and that people who wanted a puppy or another animal could call the

Farley Animal Hospital and Shelter. How did they know about all that?

Jimmy turned to Mr. Nicholson. "Did you tell the reporters?"

Mr. Nicholson's eyes sparkled. "It's part of the tale, my lad."

The phone rang about ten-thirty. Mom called, "It's for you, Jimmy. It's Blake."

He got on the phone. "Get those puppies down here, bro! People want them!"

"Now?" asked Jimmy stupidly.

"Did you see the front page of the *Tribune?* Masses of people are coming by for a Christmas pet!"

"All right!" Jimmy slammed down the phone. "Guess what?" He told his family about people wanting the puppies and the other animals.

"I can drive you to the shelter," offered Mr. Nicholson. "I could use some exercise this fine morning."

It was a fine morning. The pickup sputtered under the bright Christmas sky. Jimmy, Lassie, and the puppies rode with the boxer pair and the German short-haired pointer in the back.

All day people called and came to the shelter for pets. The puppies went first. Dr. Smith handed out vouchers to give free shots when the puppies were old enough. Katie and some of the other kids came over to help. Katie had brought bags of dog and cat food and they wrapped small bags of food to give to the new owners.

By dark, every animal, including the guinea pig, the rabbit, and the pot-belly pig, had been taken home for a Christmas present.

Mr. Nicholson drove Katie, Blake, and the other kids home on the peaceful, snow blanketed streets. Finally Mr. Nicholson turned down Jimmy's street.

"God did answer my prayer about adopting out the animals," Jimmy said.

"He was waiting for the right time," said Mr. Nicholson.

Jimmy chuckled. "I guess He knew what He was doing in the public relations department."

Mr. Nicholson pulled up in front of Jimmy's house. Their bright Christmas lights hung like brilliant gems from the roof and the shrubs. Even Mr. Krebs's house had strings of lights. Mr. Krebs must have put them up today. They weren't there earlier in the week. Jimmy smiled to himself. Talk about Scrooge having a change of heart! Mr. Krebs must have had a total heart transplant!

They pulled into the backyard, and Mr. Nicholson went into the shed to get Bess. Jimmy picked up Noel and stroked his fur.

When he came out of the shed, leading Bess, Mr. Nicholson said, "It's time for us to move on."

"Now? It's night. It's Christmas," Jimmy protested.

"It's the best time to travel," said Mr. Nicholson as he hitched the horse trailer to the truck. "No one on the road.

Besides, it's clearing up, see? We'll just follow the star."

Jimmy and Lassie stood in silence. So much had happened this past week. He had grown to love Mr. Nicholson. "I wish you didn't have to leave," Jimmy said, his hand on Noel's head.

"Thank you, Jimmy. I'll really miss you and Lassie. But I think we'll meet again someday, don't you?" He tipped his fedora. "Tell your parents and Sarah thank you for their wonderful hospitality."

Jimmy watched, Lassie pressing against his leg, as Mr. Nicholson drove the blue classic pickup down the street. Jimmy would miss Mr. Nicholson. He knew that Lassie would miss him too.

Jimmy glanced up. A large star—a planet?—gleamed in the sky, just ahead of the truck. Mr. Nicholson *was* following a star. The light of it filled Jimmy's eyes, dazzling him. When he blinked, the truck had turned a corner and was gone.

"Good-bye," he called. He stood for a moment wondering if that first Christmas was as peaceful and beautiful as this night. Lassie quietly sat next to Jimmy as if she also was trying to capture the moment. Jimmy bent down and ran his fingers through her long fur.

"What do you say, girl," he said softly. "Let's go in and finish celebrating the most important day of the year." Lassie barked, then Jimmy and Lassie raced to the door.